Best wishes,
Maralee Lowder

The Mortician's Revenge

by

Maralee Lowder

ISBN-10   1492992550

ISBN-13   978-1492992554

'The Mortician's Revenge' is published by Taylor Street Publishing, who can be contacted at: http:

http://www.taylorstreetbooks.com

http://ninwriters.ning.com

While the city of Dunsmuir is a real city in Northern California, and the Old Mortuary is a real building in Dunsmuir that is rumored to be much haunted and possibly to have the body of one of its tenants still hidden in its walls, all characters in this book are fictional, and any resemblance to anyone living or dead is accidental.

Chapter 1

Emily

Emily stood in the middle of Sacramento Avenue, hands on hips, her neck tipped so far back she felt a knot starting to form in it. Her gaze held steady on the looming old Victorian building.

Only one thought was in her mind - *what the hell was she going to do with the damned place?*

She sure as heck didn't want to live in it, and it was too big and too old to even think about trying to sell it, even if it didn't come with a whole slew of other problems, most prominent among them being the fact that she knew the old place was haunted - and not in a good way, either.

The dark windows in the former mortuary seemed to mock her as if the evil that lurked in its otherwise uninhabited rooms sensed her confusion, perhaps even thrived on it.

She had been so sure her dilemma would be solved when she offered the building and all of its contents to Dunsmuir's volunteer fire department. The solution seemed perfect. The fire department could use it as a training tool as they burned it to the ground, and she would be rid of the overwhelming problem Ada had left her.

Unfortunately, the fire chief had to refuse Emily's offer. The building was too close to its next door neighbor. And, even if that hadn't been the case, it was listed on the national registry as part of the town's historic district. It could not be destroyed without going through so much red tape she would probably be older than Ada's 93 years when she finally saw the last of the place.

Where was a good arsonist when you needed one?

"You look like you're about ready to take on that old eyesore, ghosts and all. Why don't you come over here and tell old Dr. Jim your problems," Jim Matthews, the town's family physician and the love of Emily's life, called to her. "Come on, I'll treat you to a cup of coffee and a pastry."

Letting out a deep sigh, she turned to the man she had come to love during one of the most trying, yet enriching, times of her life. It was because of Jim and Bill Shaw, Ada's attorney, that she had been reintroduced to the reclusive woman. If it hadn't been for the two men, she would never have been talked into being the old lady's caretaker during the last months of her life, and she would not have been left with the burden of trying to carry out Ada's last wishes.

Jim draped his arm over her shoulder, pulling her close to his body for a quick kiss on the cheek. "Things not going the way you'd hoped?" he asked as they started walking the short distance to the nearest coffee shop, the Brown Trout.

"You could say that. I should have known what the city would say about using the mortuary for a training opportunity for the volunteer firemen. It just seemed like *such* a good idea. One good fire and my problems would have been solved."

Jim picked her favorite treat from the diner's many pastries - a raspberry and blueberry cheesecake tart. Taking their coffee and pastry with them, they went outside to sit under an umbrella at one of the small outside tables. It was a lovely spring morning, the sort of day vacationers came to Dunsmuir to experience.

"I just don't know what I'm going to do with the place," Emily moaned. "I can't sell it and I won't even think about living in it. And the whole place needs so much work!"

"Yeah, and the kind of work that needs to be done won't come cheap. I bet that, other than replacing windows every year after the local brats broke them out on Halloween, nothing else has been done on it for the past fifty years. Frankly, I can't imagine how it's held up as well as it has."

"Well, thank heavens money's the one thing I don't have to worry about. Ada left behind more than enough. When Bill told me how much money there was in her trust, I almost passed out."

"You know, other than visiting her in her apartment up there on the top floor, I've never seen the inside of the old place. After we finish our coffee, why don't you give me a guided tour? I don't have any patients the rest of the afternoon. If you haven't got anything else you need to do, why not do it right now? Maybe I could help you make a list of all the things that need to be done."

She felt her stomach clench. *Take a tour of the mortuary?* She didn't know if she was ready for that. She had seen more of it than Jim had, but not all of it from top to bottom. Of course she had been in Ada's apartment. She'd spent every day for several months there while caring for the elderly woman. And, after the two women had renewed their warm relationship of many years before, they had occasionally returned to the first floor of the building, the place where Ada's husband had held services for the departed all those years ago. There was a lovely old pump organ down there that Ada played for her, just as she had when Emily was still a child.

Those had been some of the Emily's most treasured childhood moments, listening to Ada's music, and enjoying tea and cookies with her before leaving for home.

But at no time, neither during those early days, nor later when she came to be Ada's caretaker, had the old woman ever shown Emily the rest of the building. However, although she had never actually seen those rooms, Ada had told her so much about what it had been like for her when she lived there with her husband, Horace, Emily felt she knew everything about the creepy old place.

After hearing Ada's stories she was not the least bit afraid of seeing the embalming room down in the basement, the one area it would be expected she'd fear. No, what frightened her was the thought of going into the apartment on the second floor, the apartment Ada had shared with her husband.

"Come on, Emmy, let's do it," Jim urged her as her hesitation lingered on. "You've got to do it eventually, why not now? It's been almost a month since Ada passed. You can't wait forever."

Emily wanted to say that as far as she was concerned that was exactly what she would do. 'Forever' sounded almost long enough.

"Emmy? Come on, what do you say?"

She sat there for a moment, twisting the ring on her left hand that felt so new. She glanced down at it, hoping the gleam from the one karat diamond would give her the confidence she so desperately needed. There were things she needed to tell Jim, should have told him already, things that might change the way he felt about her.

What she wanted to say was that something horrible lived in that second floor apartment. She wanted to say she knew for a fact that those rooms were haunted by a wicked, wicked spirit that scared her half to death.

She wanted to tell him so bad she almost did, but she couldn't. If she told Jim what she had experienced herself, he would think she had lost her mind. She loved him so much she couldn't bear seeing the look in his eyes she had seen so often when she tried to explain to others what had happened to her.

They never understood. If she was lucky, they believed she was trying to fool them. The worst times were when she saw fear in their eyes, as if they were afraid of getting too close to her. She loved Jim too much to see that fear in his eyes - or, worse yet, a look of suspicion or even loathing.

Instead, she put what she hoped was a willing smile on her face and said, "If you insist! But don't be afraid. You do know it's haunted, right?"

She laughed, trying to make him think she thought the idea of ghosts and goblins was just as crazy as he probably did.

Jim was still laughing as they climbed the steps to the first floor, like a kid about to show how daring he was by going bravely into the unknown. "You never told me what kind of ghosts are supposed to haunt the place. Are they screachers? Or, better yet, do they drag chains around behind them?"

"No, they're grabbers," she said in a dramatic, hushed tone as she quickly reached over to grab his arm. "And what they grab, they keep!"

"Well, if you're the ghost, then I'll be more than happy to let you keep me," he said, his voice lowering as he leaned down to steal a quick kiss before she placed the key in the door.

She turned in his arms and raised her face to his. "I'll keep you, no matter what," she whispered as she slipped her arms around his neck and pulled him into a tighter embrace. "Why don't we skip this for now? I know of a far better way for us to spend the afternoon than to use it prowling through dusty old rooms."

"Why, you little tease," he laughed as he pulled away from her kiss. "Trying to tempt me, are you? Not this time, sweetheart. Right now we've got work to do. Let me have that key if you've forgotten how to use it. We're going to go in this place and pull back some drapes, open some windows - let a little fresh air in - and see if that doesn't get rid of a few spooks."

She reluctantly handed him the keys and stepped back while he worked the old lock. It took a bit of jiggling to break loose the rust of many years, and then the door was open and Jim was standing aside as he waited for Emily to enter the building she had inherited from Ada, the last mortician's wife.

Emily took a couple of steps into the lobby and stopped, allowing Jim to take in the splendor of the room. She remembered how it had affected her the first time she had entered it. Of course, she had been just a child at the time, but even now, as an adult, she couldn't help being impressed by the furnishings.

"Why, this isn't spooky at all," Jim said with awe in his voice. "It's ... all I can say is ... it's spectacular! These furnishings, the art ... Emily, you've inherited a fortune worth of antiques."

"It is a beautiful room, isn't it? I always loved being here with Ada. It just seems so empty without her."

She walked over to the settee Ada and she had sat on all those years ago when they had shared their little tea parties. Sitting down, she said, "She played the most beautiful music for me on that old pump organ. And then, when it was nearly time for me to go home, she brought us tea and cookies she had baked herself. We'd sit here and chat for a while. Those were the most beautiful days."

Jim stood by the old grandfather clock that had impressed the younger Emily so much, gazing at her, the look in his eyes filled to overflowing with love. "You look so beautiful sitting there with that expression in your eyes, like you're from a different time. All you need to complete the picture is one of those long white dresses with the waist cinched in so tight you can hardly breathe, with your hair piled on top of your head like a woman in one of those Gibson paintings. I can't, for the life of me, understand why you wouldn't want to live among all this beauty, remembering all the good times you spent with Ada. Why, it wouldn't be hard at all to turn this place into a beautiful home."

Emily looked at him with a smile. It pleased her that the man she loved understood her so well. If Horace's essence did not still linger in the house, she would love to make this place her home.

"And what about you?" she asked. "Could you see yourself living in a place like this? Don't you think that living in a former mortuary might be just the tiniest bit spooky?"

"Honey, it's just an old building. So what if it used to be a mortuary? That was then, this is now."

"You say that now," she replied. "Let's see what you say after you've seen the whole place."

"Lead on," he said with a smile. "But from what I've seen so far, I wouldn't mind living here one bit, especially if you were living here with me."

"Okay, we'll see about that. But to do this right, I think we should start from the bottom and make our way to the top. That means we need to go back outside and down to the basement. After you've checked that out you may have a very different opinion about living here."

They went back outside, leaving the front door open to let fresh air into the rooms in their absence, and down the stairs to the area where the mortuary's real work had gone on all those years before.

Emily felt her heart begin to race as she took the ring of keys from Jim and began searching for the one that would open the basement door. After several failed attempts she finally found one that turned the lock. She glanced over her shoulder at her fiancé with a question in her eyes. *Was he really sure he wanted to do this?* His smile told her he not only wanted to, he was actually looking forward to it. She smiled back at him, shaking her head gently from side to side, as if to say, *once a boy, always a boy*.

The room they stepped into was lined with coffins of all sizes and colors, ranging from simple to ornate. Emily's heart nearly broke as her gaze rested briefly on one that was clearly meant for a very small child.

Although it was a basement room, it was as tastefully decorated as the rooms above. The hardwood floors, while covered with dust from years of neglect, looked as if they might have just recently been refinished. Most of the floor was covered with a huge oriental rug in muted tones of blues and greens that must have cost a fortune when it had been purchased new.

It was clearly a room that had been used as a place where the deceased's loved ones would come to pick out the perfect coffin. It was a room of dignity and, yes, even of peace.

Stepping past Emily, Jim opened a door at the back of the room. The floor here was concrete, as were the walls. To the left were rows of shelves filled with the tools of the mortician's trade. She was shocked to see containers of chemicals still sitting there. How many years had it been since the last person had been embalmed in this room, she wondered - fifty, sixty?

"Wow, look at this," Jim said, directing her attention to the metal table off to their right. It was placed near a huge concrete sink. Emily did not want to think what fluids had gone into that sink and then down the drain.

At first she couldn't fathom Jim's fascination with the equipment he was so carefully inspecting, but then she realized his medical training would almost surely make such a find intriguing. It was a fascination she would never be able to share.

Leaving her fiancé to continue his examination, she turned her attention back to the shelving. There were two boxes sitting on an otherwise empty shelf that caught her attention. Drawing closer to them, she noted what appeared to be names written in black ink on their lids.

Suddenly realization hit her. "Oh, my God, I can't believe this!" she said with a tremor in her voice.

"What is it?"

"I may be wrong but I bet anything these boxes contain human ashes."

"No!"

"Jim, there are names on them, men's names. Come over here and look."

He stepped beside her and took one of the boxes into his hands, hefting it gently as if to tell by its weight what it contained.

"Don't shake it!" she said, shocked to the core at what they had discovered.

"You're right, Emily. These are what I would call 'pauper's urns' that apparently were never claimed. Wow, I wasn't expecting anything like this." He replaced the box on the shelf.

"What are we going to do? We can't keep people's ashes. That's just too creepy."

"I guess later, when we have more time, we'll have to go through those file cabinets." He nodded toward a bank of wooden cabinets that lined the wall next to the shelving. "Maybe we can find who they belong to and return them to their families."

"Let's get out of here," Emily suggested, turning to leave the room. "Frankly I'm just not up to continuing the tour today. I think I need something to calm my nerves. Maybe some wine would help."

"Wine? Something a lot stronger than wine sounds good to me."

* * *

It took several days for the two of them to find the heart to do it, but eventually they both felt ready to tackle the job of reuniting the ashes with their families. As it turned out, Horace may have had more than a few character flaws, but record keeping was not one of them. After about an hour of searching through the files, Emily and Jim found what they were looking for.

Fortunately, the first family was not at all difficult to find. They had been living in Dunsmuir for three generations and the current patriarch of the family still lived in the original home. He was amazed to discover that his great-uncle's ashes had never been retrieved, and he and the remaining members of the family were gratified that they were able finally to put their ancestor's ashes to rest.

Delivering the second box was a bit more complicated. Diligent digging through County records meant that Jim was finally able to track down a direct descendent of the deceased. Pleased with himself to have even traced a current phone number, he placed the call, looking forward to at last setting things to rest.

The response he received was not at all what he anticipated.

"How dare you call me like this!" was the elderly man's immediate response to the news that his father's ashes had been found at the old Dunsmuir mortuary. "What is this, some kind of prank?"

Jim assured him that he was definitely not trying to play any kind of prank. All he was doing was trying to do what was right.

The old man, however, was not having any of it. He was mad as hell. "Don't ever call me again!" were his final words as he slammed the phone down on the receiver.

Jim thought he had heard the last of the matter, but several days later he was surprised to see a very contrite gentleman standing in his office doorway. The story he told to Jim and Emily was even more astonishing.

"Mother and father never had much of a loving relationship," he explained, "so, when he went away and never came back, it didn't come as much of a surprise. Mother told us he was a no-good bastard who took off, leaving us all to fend for ourselves. But what I could never understand was how he could have gone and left my sister and me without ever saying a word to either of us. Mother told us that any man who would up and abandon his family like he had was nothing worth thinking about. She was a mean-hearted woman, but I would never have thought her to be so cold-hearted as to tell her own children such a cruel lie. She'd led us to believe he'd abandoned us, when all the time his ashes were right here." Tears slipped down his wrinkled cheeks as he said, "Now I can finally bring him home. And damn my mother to hell for causing so much pain to all of us."

Chapter 2

Several days slipped by after they found the gruesome surprise in the basement, with neither Emily nor Jim reminding the other they had yet to complete the tour of the old mortuary, and as each day passed, the idea of returning to the building weighed heavier and heavier on Emily's mind.

She knew Jim was right that she needed to get the ordeal over with, and the best way for her to do that would be with the man she loved at her side, but working up the necessary courage was turning out to be more difficult than she had anticipated. Did he think her a coward for putting it off, she wondered, as she let more and more time pass.

Finally, berating herself for the coward she knew she was, she invited him to join her the following Sunday - the one day of the week Jim was the least likely to be busy with a patient - for another foray into the dark recesses of her inheritance.

It was a bright, early summer day, the type of day that made living in the Northern California mountain town a true joy, and Jim had dressed appropriately in khaki shorts, a white tee-shirt and leather sandals. They met for coffee first, and after Emily had devoured two fabulous pastries and fortified herself with a half pot of coffee, they strolled hand-in-hand toward their destination.

"Do you really think you're ready for this?" Jim asked as they reached the steps of the building. Ever since they'd found the abandoned ashes he'd felt guilty about pressuring her into visiting that basement even the first time around.

"As ready as I'll ever be."

The waver he heard in her voice did little to relieve his conscience.

"You know, I've been thinking. Maybe the ghosts Ada said haunted the place came from those two men whose ashes we found. Being abandoned by their families might have really pissed them off. Hell, if it had been me boxed away like that for all those years, forgotten by everyone I loved, I might have been mad enough to do a little haunting myself."

Emily smiled at him, shaking her head slowly from side to side. She wasn't buying that one. Still, if there was anyone who would make her feel safe inside the mortuary, it would be Jim.

She unlocked the front door and stepped inside.

After checking out the rooms on the reception floor, rooms that were both beautiful and peaceful, she realized it was time for her to put away her fears and go where she most dreaded. It was the part of the building Ada had told Emily was where the evil spirit lived. It was where Horace Carpenter had brought his young bride so many years before. It was where they had lived together in disharmony, where their child had died - *and where Ada had murdered her husband.*

Emily started to tell Jim about what she had experienced the night she had first met Ada.

It was Halloween and she had been only nine years old. She and her friends had gone out trick-or-treating and ended their evening by 'tricking' the old lady at the mortuary by throwing a rock at one of the windows up here on this floor. When they heard the sound of shattering glass, all of the kids had turned tail and run - all of them except for Emily. She'd simply stood there, gazing up at what they had done, frozen to the spot by fear and shame. She had not actually thrown the rock - that was something she would never have done - but she had been there when it happened, so in her mind that made her as guilty as the girl who had actually done it.

She had expected to get into a whole lot of trouble. What she had not expected was what actually happened. As she'd stood there gazing up at the gaping hole in the window, a putrid gas began to spill out of it. Not only was the stuff the color of pea soup, it had an odor that smelled like the worse puke imaginable.

The fumes spilled over the broken glass, then flowed down the outside of the building. As she watched in horror, it began billowing toward her until she was fully enveloped by it, gagging on the horrible stench as she waved her arms at it, trying to make it go away.

Right about then the old lady who lived there had placed a board over the window, staunching the flow of horrid fumes. In mere moments it was all over. The stench disappeared, as did all other traces of her terrible experience.

It was the night Emily and Ada first became aware of one another. It was the night that the two communicated with one another telepathically, which was a first-ever experience for Emily. She had often been able to read other people's minds, but it was the first time she had ever met anyone who could do the same to her, and then actually place their thoughts into her own mind. And it was also the night the little girl realized there were some things in the world that were too horrible to comprehend.

She had never told anyone about that night, not even Jim. She was ashamed to admit she had never told him about any of her special abilities, although she knew she would have to eventually. After all, they were to be married soon. It would be wrong of her to marry him without being completely open about who she was.

But just thinking about having that conversation tied her stomach in a knot. She'd seen how people reacted to her after they'd learned she was psychic. It was never the same after that. Some of her friends had even reacted like she was in league with the devil.

"Another lock. Damn! I've never seen a house with so many locks," Jim groaned as he began trying key after key. Finally, after he'd gone through seven keys, he had success. He held open the door to Ada and Horace's old apartment and waited for Emily to precede him into the room.

After taking a big gulp of air into her lungs and releasing it with so much force that she drew a questioning look from Jim, she stepped into what turned out to be a rather ordinary, if quite dated, kitchen. She stood there for a moment, waiting for something out of the ordinary to happen to her, but nothing did. There wasn't even any odor she could detect other than that of a room that had been closed up for so many years.

She took a few more steps into the room. She was at least expecting the air to be heavily charged with Horace's terrible energy, but surprisingly, what she felt was warmth and the sense of a calm greeting. It was also as neat as a pin, as if the woman who had lived there had just stepped out after giving it a thorough cleaning.

Curious, Emily began opening cupboards and what she found in them did shock her. Shelf after shelf was packed with groceries.

Pulling out a box of cereal, she was fascinated by its vintage label. It was something she should have anticipated, yet her mind had simply not gone there. Actually, she had never given a thought as to what Ada had done when she deserted the apartment. If asked, she would have said that she supposed Ada had cleaned everything out. But that would have been something a woman who cared about the apartment might have done. Emily had forgotten just how frantically her friend had vacated the rooms all those years ago.

Jim began moving from room to room, drawing drapes aside, opening windows, allowing the fresh summer air to flow into the long abandoned rooms. "I'm not feeling any ghosts yet, are you?" he asked, a teasing note in his voice.

Stepping into the dining room, she smiled back at him as she replied, "Not so far."

She knew she sounded distrustful but vowed to try to keep an open mind about what they might find. Maybe Jim had been right after all when he attributed the ghost stories to the ashes, or maybe Horace's spirit had left the building when Ada had passed away. After all, it was she who had murdered him - why would he want to stay here if she was no longer there for him to torment?

Jim continued on ahead of Emily, checking out room after room. Every now and then she could hear him as he exclaimed at the many wonders he found. Emily could understand his astonishment. After all, he had only seen the rooms in the attic apartment where Ada had chosen to spend the last fifty years of her life. Although those rooms had been decently furnished, they were nothing compared to what he was seeing now.

Emily remembered Ada saying that one of the things in the marriage Horace had been especially pleased about was that her mother frequently gifted the young couple with expensive decorative items. As she toured the rooms, she began to understand how truly costly those gifts must have been. As pricey as those items had been when they had originally been purchased, they must be worth a fortune in today's market.

"Hey, Emily! You've got to see the neat stuff I just found."

Following Jim's voice, Emily left the living room and walked down the hallway toward the bedrooms. She did not find him until she reached the very last room - Horace's room, if she remembered Ada's description correctly.

The sight that met her eyes when she stepped into the room hit her with such a force it drove her back into the hallway.

The room was in complete disarray: clothes were strewn everywhere; a man's pants, shirt and underwear lay on the floor where they had been tossed down over fifty years before. One shoe lay by the door, the other up against the wall, as if they had been cast aside carelessly, one by one.

But it was the bed that corroborated the story Ada had told her, the story of how the abused woman had murdered her husband. The bedspread lay on the floor in a heap at the foot of the bed. The blanket and sheets were a tangled mess. And there, on the pillow at the top of the bed, was an indentation made by what could only have been a man's head.

Every aspect of the room fitted with how it would look after someone had died in agony of multiple black widow spider bites, just as Ada had described.

"Well? What do you think?" Jim asked with a huge grin as he slowly made a full circle turn before her. With a vintage leather jacket over his tee shirt and a hat from an era fifty years in the past, he should have appeared comical, but the vision Emily saw standing before her was as far from amusing as it could be.

The man she saw standing before her bore no resemblance to the man she loved.

This man's eyes bore into her soul with pure, unadulterated hatred, and rather than smiling at her, his teeth were bared as if at any moment he would lunge at her and rip her throat out.

Without ever having seen a photo of Horace Carpenter, Emily knew she was gazing at him now.

"I … I …" She felt herself begin to sway just before everything went black.

* * *

Emily felt the cool, moist compress on her forehead and Jim's tender arms cradling her as she slowly regained consciousness. The soothing tone of her fiancé's voice calmed her fluttering heart, encouraging her to force herself back to the real word.

"My God, Emmy, what happened?"

She wanted to reassure him, but when she opened her eyes, what she saw made that impossible. Once again her eyes fluttered closed. This time she tightened them, willing herself to make the vision of Horace Carpenter disappear.

"Emmy, tell me what's wrong!" Jim's voice held an edge to it she'd never heard before.

"Those clothes," she forced herself to whisper the words. "I can't look at them. They're ... oh, my God, that jacket, the hat ... they belonged to Ada's husband. I can't bear seeing you wearing anything that belonged to that animal."

She waited for a few moments as she listened to the sounds of Jim removing the offending jacket and hat, before opening her eyes once again. This time what she saw warmed her heart. Her own sweet Jim had returned to her. But from the expression she read on his face, she realized she had put off telling him her secret for far too long. It was time she opened up to the man she would soon marry. He deserved to know everything about the woman with whom he would share his life. And she deserved to know if she would be that woman.

It was time for her to admit that what she had seen as she stepped into that room was not just her Jim wearing a dead man's clothes; what she had seen was Horace Carpenter standing there, taunting her with his evil eyes and an "I've got you now" grin on his face.

Chapter 3

At Emily's suggestion, the two of them returned to her family home. She had been so happy there in the years before her mother had decided to divorce her father that she was usually able to put her troubled thoughts aside whenever she stepped into the house. Once again, as she allowed Jim to help her to her favorite chair, the house did its magic.

She leaned back into the well-worn cushions and a warm calmness settled over her. She closed her eyes and took in a soothing breath of air, then slowly bringing her head forward, she opened her eyes and released her breath. "We need to talk," she said.

"Well, maybe," Jim responded, "but before we talk I think you need a glass of wine. Something in that house gave you quite a fright. A glass of red wine will help settle your nerves."

When he returned from her kitchen with two glasses of wine in hand, she looked at him with a sad smile on her lips. She had never known she could love a man the way she did Jim. Losing him now because of what she was about to tell him would break her heart. Was she to come this close to happiness just to lose it?

"You weren't the only one who was scared to death. I may be a doctor but having the woman I love faint in my arms is not something I'm accustomed to and, believe me, it's not something I ever *want* to get accustomed to." He handed her one of the glasses and took a seat directly across from her on the sofa. "When you're ready …" he said as he sipped from his glass.

She could see by the troubled expression in his eyes that he wasn't certain he wanted to hear what she was about to tell him. She just hoped her confession would not be too much for him to handle.

"You were standing in the room where Horace Carpenter died. When I stepped into it, I didn't see you, I saw Horace."

"Well, sure you did. I was wearing his clothes."

"No, you don't understand. The man I saw was not you. I saw the real Horace. He was as real to me as you are now."

He had no answer to that statement. He just sat there staring at her, his brow knotted with confusion.

"I'm psychic, Jim. That is, I see things and hear things other people can't. Sometimes I even know things are going to happen before they do. I … well … I guess you could say I'm a bit of a weirdo."

She waited for him to respond, but all he did was sit there as if he were waiting for her to say something more. Time stretched on until he finally broke the silence by asking, "Is that it? Is that supposed to be some kind of terrible affliction or something?"

"Well, yeah, it can be."

"Can you read minds?"

"Sometimes, but most of the time I block out other people's thoughts."

"Have you ever read mine?"

She smiled at him, a teasing sort of smile. "I have you worried, don't I?"

"Well, not exactly, but ..."

"No, Jim, I have not read your mind. I respect your privacy too much to do that. I respect everyone's privacy, actually. Now that I've learned how to turn it off, I pretty much never hear anyone's thoughts except for when I'm around someone who I call a loud thinker. And then I can't help it. But you'd be surprised what dull thoughts those people usually have."

She was relieved when he began to laugh. Maybe he wasn't like so many of the people she'd had to deal with for most of her life. Maybe he would be able to accept her as she was.

"Hey, I remember hearing that some people with psychic abilities can be natural healers. You know, the 'laying on of hands' thing. Can you do that? It might be a real help with my work."

"Sorry, doctor, I'm afraid you'll just have to keep on being the healer in the family. So you're all right about me? I mean, I haven't freaked you out too much?"

He put his empty wine glass down on the coffee table and, kneeling before her, he reached out both hands and captured her face between them as he leaned in for a long, gentle kiss. "Nothing about you is going to change the way I feel about you, Emily Dawson. Why would you think something like that would make any difference in my feelings toward you?"

"You can't imagine how some people have treated me when they found out about me. I've known people who have actually called my so-called gifts 'tools of the devil'! You'd be amazed how cruel people can be to someone like me. There were times when I was just a little kid that parents stopped letting their children play with me after they found out what I could do. Eventually I hid my 'episodes', as my mother called them, from everyone. Heck, even my own mom didn't want anyone to know her little girl was so different from everyone else."

"Well, I think it's pretty neat," Jim told her between kisses. "You can tell my fortune any time you want."

"No fortune telling!" She laughed as she rose from the chair so she could draw him closer to her. "Just lots and lots of this," she promised as she stepped into his embrace before drawing back again. "I have one more thing to say about all of this spooky stuff and then I don't want to talk about it anymore." Her tone had lost its playfulness. Her next words were spoken in a voice that made it quite clear she would brook no argument about what she was saying. "I don't want to ever go into that building again and I want you to promise me you won't go in there, either."

"But …"

"No, I mean it. Neither one of us. *Ever.*"

Chapter 4

Emily could not remember ever having been so happy, or so busy, as she was during the next few months. In addition to planning their wedding, she and Jim set out on a fervid search to find the perfect home to return to after their honeymoon. Although Emily loved the house her father had left her, it was too small for the life they hoped to share - one filled with children and friends - and, unfortunately, Jim's house was even smaller than hers.

Until the moment she had seen Horace looking at her through her fiancé's eyes as they toured the old mortuary, they had been considering making that old building their home. In many ways it would have been perfect: it had been designed by the famed architect, Julia Morgan, who had built Hearst Castle at San Simeon and Wyntoon for William Randolph Hearst, and its bones were fantastic. With six bedrooms and five bathrooms, there was no way they would ever outgrow it. It may once have been a mortuary, but as Jim pointed out, that was simply part of the building's unique history.

And in spite of her misgivings, Emily had wanted to believe what he said to be true. She had even been on the verge of agreeing with him until that moment she saw him standing in Horace's bedroom, wearing his jacket and hat. What she saw then made her vow to never step foot in the building again. The man she saw in that room was not her Jim. By simply entering the room and donning Horace's clothing, Jim had called forth the monster who had lived there so many years before. The hatred that had glared from his eyes had hit her at gut level. What she saw was a man so evil that, if he was released from the room, no one would ever be safe.

The day after that horrible experience Emily contacted a local real estate broker and she and Jim both put their homes on the market to begin the search for a home they could share for the rest of their lives. At Jim's suggestion, Emily inspected each prospective house using not only her normal senses but also her own special gift. They were determined to find a home with an energy that matched their own - a house filled only with happy memories.

The house they chose was probably as old as the mortuary but held none of its painful memories. It was a two-story Victorian with both an attic and a basement. The large lot was filled with flower beds and fruit trees.

When Emily noted a child's swing hanging from the limb of a gnarly old apple tree, she felt her heart melt. It was in that moment that she knew she had found the home where she and Jim would spend the rest of their lives. With the vision of children swinging from that tree, not only their children but their grandchildren as well, she entered the house for the first time, knowing in her heart that she need look no further.

They bought the house immediately and her subsequent days were spent either working on it or on the details of their upcoming wedding. No matter what she was doing, either painting a wall or ordering flowers for the wedding, it seemed her heart was singing with happiness. As each day passed she felt she was falling more and more in love with both her new home and the man who would soon be her husband. She couldn't imagine there ever having been a woman who was more blessed.

They both worked so hard during those weeks that time seemed to lose its meaning. One day they were painting walls and sanding hardwood floors, and the next day they were attending their wedding rehearsal dinner. The day after that they would be married and on the way to their honeymoon.

Chapter 5

It was a picture-perfect wedding. The weather had cooperated beautifully, with a temperature in the mid-70s, just a few fluffy white clouds and a whisper-light breeze. As she walked along the garden path toward her future husband, her veil floated lightly over the glistening dark brown curls that brushed her shoulders. The veil ended just below her chin in the front, with a long flowing expanse of delicate lace at the back. It was anchored to her head with a simple, yet elegant, pearl-encrusted band. Her gown, rather than being icy white, which before she entered the bridal salon she had been sure she wanted, ended up having a rich, creamy pearl tone.

It seemed that everything she had envisioned all her life for her wedding had changed. Instead of the cathedral wedding she had dreamed of, the aisle she walked down was a garden path. Instead of choosing the princess-style dress of her dreams, she had chosen an elegantly tailored gown. And the reality was far surpassing anything she had ever imagined.

As Emily walked alongside Paul, the man she had learned to love more as a friend than as the stepfather he was, the strangest thing happened. There, at the end of the path, standing beneath a flower-covered arch, stood the man with whom she would spend the rest of her life. He was a nice enough looking guy, but who the heck was he? What did she really know about him? What had she been thinking when she had agreed to spend the rest of her life with this man who was little more than a stranger?

If it hadn't been for Paul's sturdy grip on her arm, she would have stumbled, and maybe even turned around and fled. Feeling a desperation she had never known before, she glanced at Paul who responded to her panicked expression by whispering, "Feeling a little scared? Don't worry, sweetheart, it's just wedding day jitters." But still the urge to escape was threatening to overpower her.

Emily returned her attention to the man who was waiting for her at the altar, the man she loved with all her heart. Now it was her Jim who stood there, with more love in his eyes than she could have ever hoped for. Ignoring the fear that had so suddenly gripped her, she gazed into his eyes and smiled. She couldn't wait to join him at the altar.

After the weeks, or rather months, Emily had spent planning the reception, she could not say she actually enjoyed it. She was certain the caterer had done a superb job, since she heard nothing but positive comments about the food, but she couldn't remember eating one bite. That was, of course, with the exception of the fork full of cake Jim carefully placed in her mouth.

She had made him promise he would not partake in that utterly ridiculous common practice of the groom smashing wedding cake all over the face of the woman he had just promised to love and to cherish. She had told him how she felt about it, how the act of demeaning the person you had just vowed to love for all time by smearing food all over their face was nothing short of mean-spirited. As far as she was concerned, making a fool of the one you loved was just about as far from a loving gesture as anyone could imagine.

However, she would not have put it past him to succumb to this firmly established tradition among his old school friends. There was not one among them who had been known to pass up an opportunity to make the others laugh. From the stories she had heard about his friends' wedding receptions, she had fully expected Jim to follow in their footsteps.

Her head swam as group after group of well-wishers approached her. She would never be able to recall how many people held her in tender embraces while whispering their expressions of good will, nor how many men felt it their duty to kiss the bride. So much was happening at once she frequently had to remind herself to try to remember every single moment, although she knew that was an impossible task. It was just so much! All those weeks and months of planning, all the tiny details to remember. It was a wonder anyone ever got married. If only they had eloped ...

As the sun began to slip behind the nearest hill, the band packed up their instruments and the lingering guests bid the bridal couple their final farewells. Emily sighed with relief, thanking God it was finally over and she and her husband would be able to get back to real life.

"Come on, sweetheart, let's get the honeymoon started!"

With those simple words Jim managed to break through all the craziness and stabilize her. It was time to forget everything except each other. The wedding, the reception, all of it had been more for their guests than themselves. It was only the vows they had sworn to each other that truly mattered - the vows and the *honeymoon*.

Just thinking about the trip they were about to embark upon brought a smile to her lips. They were to drive down to San Francisco, where they would board a cruise ship the next morning for seven full days of cruising south to Mexico. Seven days with nothing to do but to enjoy each other.

Part Two

Spahn Ranch

Chapter 6

Eddy Sudcliff had the world by the horns, and he knew it. He took a deep draw on his joint, held the singeing smoke deep in his lungs for as long as he could before slowly expelling it.

Wearing beat-up old cowboy boots, frayed Levis and a faded blue plaid flannel shirt, he might have been mistaken for one of the ranch hands, but his status on the old Spahn Movie Ranch was far less defined. He had simply shown up one day and hadn't gotten around to leaving yet.

It was a pleasant enough location in the rugged Southern California foothills, away from the city yet close enough that a guy could always get into town for a bit of entertainment or a refill of his stash, but Eddy didn't figure he'd stay there forever. It was one of those places you dreamed about when you were a kid, enjoyed for a while when you got there, and then left to journey on to check out other dreams.

He'd never heard of the Spahn Ranch before Charlie Manson's blood-thirsty gang killed Sharon Tate and all those other people. That was when Eddy first learned about the place where so many of his favorite Western films had been shot. The murder scenes were so shocking the newspapers couldn't print enough about the perpetrators.

It really bummed him out when he thought of how the Manson Family had used the Beatles' song 'Helter Skelter' as an excuse to go crazy like they had. It was a damned sacrilege, that's what it was. The Beatles, they were gods, for Christ's sake! You don't just go and do something like that and say the Beatles made you do it. It just wasn't right.

He hated what those dumb hippies had done and all, but he couldn't help being intrigued with everything he read about the ranch they called home in the days leading up to the murders. It played on his mind so much that when he'd had enough of going to college classes that totally bored him, he decided it was a good time to check the Spahn Ranch out for himself.

He had been thinking about dropping out of school even before he'd screwed up his finals, but the thought of leaving Southern California always held him back. In the entire twenty-two years of his life he had never lived more than fifteen miles from the ocean. From the time he was old enough to carry a board, surfing had been his life. The thought of never riding another wave, of never feeling sprays of salty water splash over his body, and of never seeing bikini-clad babes displaying themselves on the sand, always kept him from acting on his impulse to leave the coast behind to explore the rest of the world.

That was until he screwed up and flunked all but one of his mid-terms. That was when he figured his decision had been made for him. It wasn't as though he'd be welcomed back at home with open arms and loving smiles. Not very likely.

He didn't have to go home to know what his parents would say. He could hear it in his head, "Get a haircut. Buy some decent clothes. Get a damned job, for God's sake."

When he'd made up his mind to leave school, he hadn't wasted any time clearing out his bank account and buying an old VW bus, strapping his favorite surfboard to the top of it, and then stuffing all the rest of his belongings in the back. Not having any clear plan for his future other than smoking more hash and screwing more babes, he figured he might as well just take off and see what life had to offer.

He figured he probably should have let his parents know what he was doing, leaving school and all that, but hell, they'd never cared a whole lot about what he was doing for most of his life - why should things be any different now? They'd always been too busy with their careers to bother with him. And, when they weren't working, they were traveling all over the world, trying to "get in touch with real people." Sometimes he'd wondered what he could do to become one of those people - the people they found so much more interesting than their own son.

When he finally arrived at the ranch, he had not been disappointed. It was just how he had imagined it, but even better. Walking past those old buildings he had seen in so many of his favorite Westerns made him feel that he had stepped into those films. Whereas someone else might hear nothing more than the wind chasing tumbleweeds, Eddy heard the voices of cowboys, gun fighters and a whole cast of other Western characters. The wind-driven dust devils that swept down the dirt street of the western village, catching him in swirls of gritty sand, anchored him in a new reality.

He hadn't been at the ranch long before he began to get really pissed-off about how old George Spahn was being treated. The press made the old man sound like he was part of what those bastards had done, which just wasn't true. He was a decent man who deserved better than he got. All the poor guy had done was to offer a bunch of hippies a place to stay for a while. How the hell was he to know how everything was going to turn out?

The cops weren't much better than the press. Eddy arrived at the ranch weeks after the murders, yet the place was still crawling with cops and reporters. From what the other guys on the ranch told him, Mr. Spahn had cooperated completely with the search, yet most of the pigs treated the poor guy like he had been part of Hitler's inner circle. It just wasn't fair.

Eddy cared a lot about the old man and the rest of the people who worked on the ranch. Even after all that was going on around them, they had been nothing but decent to him when he'd come driving up to their door, asking for a place to stay. He'd halfway expected to be sent packing before he got out of his bus, but they'd treated him okay and he appreciated it.

And although he'd never so much as done one day of manual labor in his life before arriving there, he found he enjoyed working with the ranch hands. Oh, sure, they enjoyed making him the butt of their jokes but wasn't that the way it should have been? In every Western he'd ever seen there'd always been the guy the others gave a hard time, just because he was new on the job. There was never any meanness in their jokes, just a way to get a good laugh from the rest of the crew. It gave him a feeling he had never known before, that of belonging.

But it was getting on to time for him to go, time for him to find out what else was out there waiting for him.

Sometimes in the evenings, when the rest of the guys were settling down after a good meal, Eddy would wander from one old building to another, letting the place take him back to when he was just a kid and going to the movies he had lived for. He liked it best at twilight when the shadows began to creep over the ranch. He'd walk from building to building, imagining a pair of six shooters strapped to his thighs, the sound of spurs jingling as he took each step. He could almost hear the forlorn sound of a harmonica playing a slow, mournful tune as he took one deliberate step after another.

He had come to love the place but knew in his heart he couldn't stay. The ranch would be one of those places he would remember forever, always longing to return, yet never being able to. Some places were meant for the moment, and for him the Spahn Ranch was one of those places. He might come back some day, but most likely wouldn't.

He drew in a deep breath of thin, clean air. That was part of the problem, he decided. Having grown up in San Diego surfing nearly every day, he missed air that had a little substance to it. He missed the taste of salt and smelling the fumes coming from crowded freeways. Hell, who was he kidding? He missed the babes! Yeah, maybe it was time for him to load the old bug up and head on out.

He'd been hearing a lot about Haight Ashbury up in San Francisco for a long time now. Maybe that was where he should go. Hell, he wouldn't mind connecting up with some of the free love he'd been hearing so much about, especially if it was true it came with some really good hash.

He rose from his place on the old building's wooden porch. Stretching to his full six foot three height, he let himself dwell on the idea of having one of those flower children under each arm. He smiled as he pictured long-haired girls cuddling up to him and smiling seductively at him as they held fragrant flowers under his nose. He was a good looking guy and he knew it. He'd most likely have a whole harem of women after him. He'd seen pictures of what those hippie guys looked like - long, dirty hair and beads down to their navels. Hell, most of the guys he'd seen in the newspaper photos looked like a bunch of skinny wimps. All he'd have to do would be to let the women see what a real man looked like and he'd have all the pussy he could handle.

He didn't have to look in a mirror to know he'd make all those other guys look like nature's rejects. What girl wouldn't pick a cool surfer dude over those guys? Yeah, his blond sun-streaked hair was long, but not like those other guys. His was cool, always clean and actually styled. Thanks to his parents' constant pursuit of perfection, his teeth were brilliantly white and could not have been straighter. The complete package of height, well-muscled body, golden tan, blue eyes, etc., etc., etc., made him a perfect female magnet.

The vision of himself with more women than he could handle helped him make up his mind. First thing in the morning he was going to pack up his stuff, throw it into his VW bus and hit the road. It was time.

He threw the last bit of his joint onto the dirt, ground it out with the heel of his boot, and headed over to the bunk house in search of some food - any food. Damn he was hungry!

Chapter 7

The sun's heat was just beginning to envelop the ranch as Eddy turned his bus west on his way to meet up with highway 101 at Ventura. He knew he wouldn't feel he had actually begun his next adventure until he could see the Pacific Ocean once again. He could barely wait to see it lose itself on the far horizon as he traveled north along the celebrated highway.

He pulled to the side of the road and lit up a joint in celebration of the beginning of a new adventure. He turned his radio on, played with the dial until he found a station playing Jefferson Airplane, and settled back into his seat.

* * *

By the time he reached San Lois Obispo he was so ravenous he pulled into the parking lot of the first diner he saw. Consumed with visions of a hamburger dripping with fat and mayo, a heaping pile of fries and a couple of milks - one vanilla, the other chocolate - he barely noticed the thin girl who stood outside the restaurant's doorway. He might not have noticed her at all if she had not moved to stand outside the window of the booth where he sat.

He could barely tolerate his hunger as he waited, first for the waitress to take his order, then for his food to reach his table. It wasn't until he had bolted down half of the burger and one of the shakes that he took notice of the girl glancing at him through the glass. After he'd seen her look at him for the third time, he let himself be drawn into her gaze. He wasn't all that impressed with what he saw.

She looked to be about eighteen - just barely legal. Her ankle-length skirt and oversized blouse hid any figure she might have. She had on a slouchy brown hat that kept her face in shadow but did not hide the length of her sandy blond hair. The bulging duffle bag that rested at her feet suggested she might be one of those hippie girls he'd been dreaming about, one of the 'flower power people,' as the papers had daubed them.

That thought made him give her a second glance. Yeah, she sure looked like a hippie. Were all female hippies flower children, he wondered? And, more important, were they all into that free love stuff?

On a whim, he called the waitress over to his table and ordered a duplicate of his original order, this time in take-out containers. Not even thinking of leaving a tip, he picked up the food and left the restaurant.

"Hey, could you give a girl a ride?"

Her voice gave him a bit of a start. It was nothing like he had imagined. He'd figured flower children would all sound kind of dreamy, like little kids. But this hippie's voice was gravelly, like she'd been smoking too many cigarettes, or more likely joints. There was nothing girlish about her voice at all.

"Sure," he said. "Which direction are you going?"

"Does it matter?"

"If it doesn't matter to you, I guess it doesn't matter to me."

"You going to eat all that food yourself?"

"I wasn't planning on it. What I was planning was giving you both a ride *and* the food."

"Okay."

"Just *okay*? Don't you even want to know what direction I'm heading?"

"Not really," she said as she reached out for the bag with the burger and fries.

And that was how Eddy met Valerie, or as she preferred to call herself, 'Aries.'

They rode in silence as she wolfed down her meal. When she announced that she had finished her second shake by making loud sucking noises as she reached the bottom of the container, Eddy wondered if he should have bought her a strawberry one, too.

After expelling a very satisfying burp, she asked, "So where are we going, anyway? Oh, yeah, and what's your name?"

"I'm headed up to Frisco - thought I'd take in a bit of that flower power stuff they got going up there. And, to answer your second question, my name is Eddy Sudcliff."

"I hate to tell you, 'Eddy Sudliff', but flower power is all but over."

"And you would know because ..."

"Cuz I was there when it was good. Now it's just a bunch of hippie want-a-bes. The pigs chased off everyone who was real."

Her answer was not what he wanted to hear. If not San Francisco, then where?

"So, what's your name, anyway?" he asked, not so much because he cared, but more to change the subject so he could give the question of whether he still wanted to go to San Francisco or not some thought.

"I go by Aries."

"You mean you are an Aries, don't you? No one names a kid after a sign of the Zodiac."

"I can go by any name I want, and I go by my sign."

"Okay, then I guess that makes me Leo, since that's my sign."

"If ya want'a."

The unsaid words that let him know she really didn't care what he called himself brought an end to the conversation.

Sated by her meal, Aries drew her left foot up onto the seat, bringing her knee nearly to her chin. With her right foot still on the floor board, her skirt was stretched to its fullest. She leaned her back against the passenger door so she now faced Eddy full-on. With her head tipped back, she kept her half-closed eyes pinned on him.

He couldn't keep his gaze from drifting to the hem of her skirt. From where he was sitting he could see she hadn't wasted any money on underwear. He forced his gaze back to the road. Did she realize what she was doing?

When he shot a glance back at her, this time directly into her eyes, he had his answer. Oh, yeah, she knew exactly what she was doing.

"Uh, yeah … um, I've been driving for a long time. Kind'a getting tired. What do you say we call it a day and check into the next motel we come to?"

"I thought you'd never ask." Her smile broadened. Anyone other than a very horny male could not have missed the expression of satisfaction on her face. She knew exactly what she wanted, and she knew exactly how to get it.

The motel room was about as tacky as it could get. Nothing had been done to conceal the spots on the orange shag carpet where it had been worn down to the threads. Hooks that held up water-stained turquoise and lime green curtains were missing here and there, giving the impression of a gapped-toothed grin. Eddy wasn't much into interior decorating but even he wondered how anyone might have thought the pink and green flowered bedspread belonged anywhere within a mile of the curtains *or* the orange carpet.

Apparently Aries was not overly concerned one way or another over the tacky decorations. As soon as she stepped into the room, she headed straight to the bathroom, carrying her duffle bag with her. In a few moments Eddy heard the toilet flush and then the sound of water running in the shower.

"The bathroom's all yours," Aires said a few moments later as she walked out of the room, a scanty towel just barely covering her nakedness. She was trying to make a sarong out of it by tucking one corner inside the other, without success. With a grimace indicating she'd accepted the fact that there simply was not enough towel to complete the job even though she was thin to the point of emaciation, she let it drop to the floor, as she casually walked to the bed.

She stepped past him as if he wasn't even there, completely comfortable with her nakedness. Treated to a full-frontal view of her, he noted her small breasts and the trim triangle of dark blond hair at the apex of her legs. As she reached up to straighten the towel she had wrapped around her hair, he observed that neither her legs nor her armpits had seen a razor in a very long time.

It put him off a bit. In what he now regarded as his former life, the women he had slept with had always been impeccably groomed. Were all the flower children so ... natural?

" 'Course you don't have to take a shower if you don't want to. You're the guy that paid for this dump. You can use it however you want." She said the last words as she threw the wildly printed bedspread onto the floor. She pulled the blanket aside and slipped between the sheets.

Wondering if, since he had fed her and paid for the room, she felt it was okay for him to use *her* however he wanted was also as part of the deal, he headed toward the bathroom. With only a slight feeling that something was wrong with what he was doing, he closed the bathroom door and turned on the shower. He waited for the water to warm up, patiently at first, and then not so patiently. Great, apparently she'd used up all the hot water.

What the hell, he thought as he stepped into the cool stream. He ought to just go out there and fuck her without the shower. But that was not his habit, and he almost always stuck with his habits. He was a guy who liked habits. They took away the need to think things through. And he was also a guy who spent as little time thinking as possible.

He was chilled to the bone when he stepped out of the shower. He tried to dry himself with one of the scratchy towels provided by the motel, but eventually gave up, choosing to let his body air dry rather than to rub himself raw. He tried to hide the fact that he was shivering from head to toe when he reentered the bedroom.

Aries was sitting up, with the headboard at her back, waiting for him as he stepped back into the room. Locking her gaze with his, she tipped her chin up in a motion of assent.

He stopped shivering immediately. "How about a joint?" he asked, figuring it was the gentlemanly thing to do. "We don't need to rush into this, you know."

Her gaze left his face and traveled down his body until it rested on his very erect penis. "Yeah, I think a little rushing might be a good idea. We can do the joint together between session number one and session number two. Heck, who knows how many sessions we might get to if you got enough hash. "

Eddy was only good for three sessions that day. After the last one, he slept the sleep of a very satisfied man.

Chapter 8

When Eddy finally managed to pull himself out of bed late the next afternoon, he headed the bus first to the nearest diner, then back onto highway 101. From what he'd heard they were about to come to the most beautiful part of the California coast. It was a large part of his reason for making the trip, so he was anxious to see for himself what all the hype was about.

He had always been fascinated by the stories his friends in school had told about vacations they'd taken with their parents, which often included trips up the California and Oregon coasts. Their stories captivated him. First, because the idea of parents taking their children along on a vacation was something he himself had never experienced. His parents, both very successful psychiatrists, loved to travel, however the idea of their taking their son along with them apparently never occurred to them. And second, because he was fascinated by the idea that this part of the ocean might be different from any other part of the Pacific coast. He highly expected those other guys were using the fact that they had actually been allowed to accompany their parents on a vacation to taunt him. He had always planned on taking the trip himself to see if what they told him was anywhere near the truth.

"Hey, you run out of hash already?"

Aries' gravelly voice irritated him. They hadn't been on the road for more than fifteen minutes. Couldn't she forget about getting high long enough for him to get fully awake? But after remembering the night before he decided he could put up with her voice and constant need to get high if it meant more of what he'd gotten from her already.

"Check out that bag down by your feet. And look in the glove compartment for the wrappers." He thought to tell her to go ahead and roll herself a joint, but stopped when he realized Aries was apparently not someone who waited for invitations to get what she wanted.

The overly sweet scent of the smoke billowing through the cab began to make him nauseous. He rolled his window down, but that only served to suck the smoke toward him. "Want to roll down your window?" he asked, trying to keep the irritation that was building within him out of his voice.

Not bothering to respond verbally, she did as he asked. The next thing he knew she was holding the smoldering joint under his nose. "Here, take a hit. It'll make you feel better."

He took his hand off the wheel long enough to shove her offering away.

Silence settled over the inside of the vehicle as they continued their journey. Mile after mile of California's gorgeous coast passed without either of the occupants breaking the silence. Thoughts of how he could get rid of his passenger battled in his mind with the question of whether or not he really wanted to.

Glancing over at her, he wondered if she was thinking the same thing about him, but after seeing the dreamy look in her eyes, he decided she probably wasn't thinking about much of anything, much less about wanting to be back on her own.

After nearly an hour of driving, she startled him when she broke the silence. "You still figuring on going to Frisco?"

"I don't see why not."

"You're not going to like it."

"That's something I'll have to see for myself, isn't it?"

Once again silence settled over the two. They'd driven about five miles farther when Eddy saw that a rest stop was coming up. He kept silent until he entered the mini-park and pulled into a parking slot. Turning to face her, he said, "You know, you don't have to come along if you don't want to. It probably wouldn't take you long to find some other guy who would be glad to give you a ride."

"Hey! Don't get all riled up. I was just trying to keep you from being disappointed. You want to see the flower children at the Haight, then we'll go and see them – together - if the offer still stands. It's just that I heard nothing's happening there anymore. They say Oregon's the place to go. I heard pot grows wild up there."

"It might grow wild but I bet the cops aren't any different there than anywhere else. If you get nailed with it, I bet you sure as hell get as much jail time as you do down here in California."

"If you get nailed, yeah, but the thing is, the pigs up there don't care if you smoke. The rumors say the pigs like the stuff just as much as everyone else."

"Look, why don't you just get out here. I'll give you a stash and some money to keep you going, but no matter what you say, I'm going to check out the ol' city by the bay for myself." He reached down to pick up the bag of marijuana at her feet. "Here, take all of it. I can get more when I get there."

She took the sack out of his hand, then placed it back at her feet. "Naw, forget it. I'm in for Frisco, if that's how you feel about it. That is, if you still want some company."

She turned in the seat so she could spread her legs as she reached out for his hand. Smiling into his eyes, she drew his hand to her, directing his fingers into her moistness. If he had looked into her eyes without the haze of lust clouding his vision, he might have had the good sense to open her door and escort her from his vehicle. Her eyes held a knowing look that told him she was a girl who had traveled roads beyond his imagination

Her smile widened when she heard him draw in his breath. She knew he could get hash anywhere, he could even get all the sex he could handle just about anywhere, but why bother looking when he had what he needed right here?

Her smile was still in place as she climbed into the back of the bus. In moments his pants were down and her skirt was up.

Chapter 9

After leaving San Luis Obispo, Eddy turned onto Highway One, the famous road that hugged the Pacific Ocean until it ended just south of Salinas. It was a beautiful drive, far more so than he had ever imagined. Not in any hurry to end the journey, he made stop after stop along the way to enjoy the breathtaking beauty. He had never been particularly interested in photography but now he wished he had a camera. But mere photographs could never do justice to the miraculous views spread out before him.

And, even if he was able to photograph the wonders of Northern California's rugged coastline, how could he capture the mingling scents of the ocean and the redwoods. Or the sound of waves crashing over huge boulders. Only by committing it to memory would he be able to relive the mystical magic that filled his senses.

Time and again, he pulled the bus off the highway so he could get closer to an especially entrancing view. Without inviting his passenger to join him, he took solitary walks along the shore or deep into the shadows of towering trees. Time meant nothing to him as he immersed himself into his surroundings. He was solitary, yet not alone. He felt himself become a part of all he saw, smelled and heard.

He was so engrossed in his heightened senses he failed to hear the footsteps that followed him into the quiet of the woods.

"So, what are we going to do, stay here all night?" Aries voice startled him out of his reverie. As he turned to answer her, he felt as if his spirit was suddenly sucked back into his body. Before he had felt one with the universe; now he felt as if his feet had been suddenly anchored firmly to the earth.

"What?"

"I said are we going to stay here all night? It's going to get dark pretty soon. If we're going to stay we better make ourselves a camp."

The idea of camping out had never entered his mind but it sounded like a good idea. Unfortunately, since he had always lived a city sort of existence, he'd never even thought about purchasing the equipment needed for a comfortable night out in the open.

"You know what? That's not a bad idea," he said as he headed back to the bus, with her tagging closely to his heals. When they reached the bus, Aries was surprised to see that instead of beginning to unload the gear they'd need, he headed instead toward the driver's door. "Are you coming along or staying here?" he called to her as he pulled the door closed and started the motor. Not about to be left behind in the wilderness, she scampered around to the passenger side and slipped into the seat as the bus began to move.

"I thought you said camping was a good idea."

"I did."

"Then why are we leaving?"

"We're leaving so we can get to the next town and get the stuff we'll need, that's why."

"I don't get you. You drive this hippie bus, even listen to hippie music, but you sure as hell aren't much of a hippie! I've never known a hippie yet that couldn't pull off to the side of the road and set up camp, just like that." She snapped her fingers in his face. "Who the hell are you, Eddy or Leo? Are you just another hippie want'a be?

He was silent for a few moments, giving her question some serious consideration. Finally he answered. "Up until a few weeks ago, I'd have to say I was Eddy. Even now, after living at the ranch and all, and the fact that I'm on my way to the Haight, I guess who I am is still in doubt. But, if I had to pick one or the other, I'd have to say Eddy's kind'a morphing into Leo with every passing mile."

"What ranch?" The tone of her voice sounded like she really didn't care.

"I was over at the Spahn Ranch the last couple'a months. I..."

"What? You were at the Spahn Ranch? Like the Spahn Ranch where Charlie Manson lived?"

"Yeah …"

"Did you meet him?"

"Meet who? Old man Spahn?"

"I don't give a shit about the old man! Did you meet Charlie?"

He didn't like the way she spoke about Mr. Spahn. He was a good guy and did not deserve to be treated the way Charlie Manson and his gang had.

"No, I never met Manson or any of his crew. And Mr. Spahn…"

"Maybe you stayed in the same house as Charlie?"

"No. All I saw that had anything to do with the Manson family was the cops who were looking for evidence, plus the press who were all over the place like maggots on a turd. They made a real mess of everything … even more of a mess than Manson's groupies had."

"Oh, my God, did the pigs tell you anything? You know, anything that didn't make the papers? Stuff that was too gruesome to print?"

"What are you, some kind of Manson worshipper?"

"Hell, yeah, I am! Charlie, man, he was the king!"

Eddy might have expected a lot of things to come out of Aries' mouth, but the fact that she could actually idolize a guy like Charles Manson completely dumbfounded him.

"Have you ever seen a picture of him?" Without waiting for him to answer, she continued, "God! His eyes, have you ever seen his eyes?"

Shocked at her words, he glanced over at her. He found himself looking directly into her eyes … eyes that held the same maniacal expression he had seen in the newspaper photographs. She grinned at him then, and suddenly her eyes changed back to normal. Camping in the wilderness with Aries had suddenly lost its charm.

Their next stop was in Salinas, back on highway 101. There he found a source where he could replace his dwindling stash of pot.

He did not look for camping equipment.

Chapter 10

There wasn't a lot of conversation between the two of them as they continued driving north. Somewhere after they left Salinas, Aries apparently decided that trying to talk Eddy out of going to San Francisco would most likely get her left beside the road. Her reason for trying to persuade him out of going was not as important as staying with him.

When they finally arrived at the City, Eddy had to admit having Aries along for the ride had its advantages. He never would have made it through the Bay Area's maze of urban streets without her. The whole area was as confusing as the tangle of cities that made up Los Angeles County. Left to his own devices, he would have never found the street corner that had lived in his imagination for the last couple of years.

"Don't turn here!" Aries yelled just in time to keep him from turning the wrong way on a one way street. "There, at the corner with the liquor store, turn left. Go two, no, three blocks and turn right." It had been that way ever since they'd crossed into the San Francisco city limits. How the hell did anyone ever know where they were going in this crazy city?

And then they were there - the corner of Haight and Ashbury - the place that haunted his imagination.

It was not exactly what he had hoped for.

He slowed down but, since there did not appear to be a vacant parking spot anywhere in sight, did not stop. He didn't have to walk the street to see that it was nowhere like what the newspapers claimed it to be. Where were all the girls with wreaths of flowers in their hair? Where were the musicians who were supposed to be playing guitars and tambourines, sharing music of rebellion and visions of the future? Where were all the young girls dancing to the music, their faces radiating the joy of complete freedom? Where were the guys with bandana headbands and hip hugger Levis?

Aries seemed to know enough to not say, "I told you so!" Instead, she said, "Don't get all bummed out. It's too early for anything much to be going on. We'll come back later and I'll show you all the flower power you can handle."

After he had driven past the famous corner, seeing only a few down-on-their-luck juveniles panhandling from tourists who, like himself, formed a parade of vehicles, she said, "Come on, I'll show you my favorite coffee shop."

Following her directions once again, he drove until she pointed out a parking space.

The words 'coffee shop' brought up images of places he had heard about where hippies sat in darkened rooms drinking fancy European coffee and listening to Indian music. Never having been in a legitimate coffee house, he mistakenly expected coffee shops and coffee houses to be one and the same. Images of a long haired girl playing an acoustic guitar while she recited obscure but meaningful poetry pleasantly filled his mind.

He was to be disappointed once again. In place of the coffee house he had imagined, the building they approached turned out to be a rather seedy-looking diner.

"Well, it's a place to get something to eat, anyway," he mumbled as he turned with Aries to enter the eatery.

"Hey, how much money do you have on you?"

She had stopped just short of entering the building. "I mean," she lowered her voice, "do you have enough to give those two girls a burger or something? They look like they haven't had a decent meal in a long time."

Damn it. Anyway, what did she want him to do? Feed every street kid they found? Then he looked where she was pointing and knew he was lost.

They were two of the saddest looking girls he had ever seen. Both were skinny as rails. Their long dresses hung on them like they might as well have been clothes hangers. They had noticed him looking at them and were returning his gaze with dull, lusterless eyes. They looked as if they had been hungry for so long they no longer knew how to ask for help.

"Bring 'em in," he told Aries, then turned into the diner and began looking for a table for four.

When the waitress approached their table, Aries took over, ordering double-sized burgers for all four of them, along with fries and shakes. They sat in silence, waiting for their orders. When the food came, the two young girls did not simply eat the food, they attacked it. When they finished, Eddy called the waitress over and ordered a second serving for each of them.

Aries was the first to break the silence with what was to become her trademark question whenever she met someone new. "What are your signs?"

The first girl to speak appeared to be the oldest, which still could not have been over sixteen. "I'm an Aquarian."

"And I'm a Libra."

Eddy noticed that being asked their Zodiac sign before they were asked for their names did not faze either of the girls.

"Aren't you going to ask them their names? You do have names, don't you?" he asked, glancing first at one girl and then the other. They both returned his gaze with silence and dull expressions. The expression he saw on Aries' face told him how little he knew about the world all three women came from.

Resigned that he would never understand females, especially these females, he turned his attention back to the waitress. Signaling to her that he was ready for his check, he rose, dropped the money on the table and turned to leave.

"I'm going out for a smoke," he called over his shoulder.

Aries jumped to her feet and stepped quickly over to him. "You can't smoke a joint out there, right on the street!" she hissed into his ear. "I told you, it's not like that around here anymore!"

He just shook his head like he would at a very small, very annoying child. Reaching into his pocket, he drew out a pack of Camels, held it in his palm and waved it before her face. "Cigarettes are still legal around here, aren't they?"

Her obvious exasperation gave him his first laugh of the day. He was still laughing as he stood with his back to the restaurant while he lit up his smoke.

Behind his back the three young women's heads were drawn together over the table. Leaning toward the others, Aries was speaking fast. She looked first to one and then to the other, all the time speaking quickly. Neither of the others spoke. At first it appeared Aries' words were having no effect on the girls. Their expressions remained as dull as they had been when they had first sat down at the table.

But gradually, first one and then the other, their expressions began to change. A glint of understanding came to their eyes. After a few more minutes of listening to Aries' words, smiles actually emerged on both of their faces. By the time the three young women left the restaurant they were all sharing conspiratorial smiles.

"They're coming with us," was all Aries seemed to think she needed to say to Eddy.

"What the hell?"

Without bothering to respond to Eddy, Aries turned to the girls and directed them to where they would find the VW bus.

"You can't miss it," she called out to them. "It's the one with the stupid surfboard on top."

"Stupid?"

"Oh, don't bother about that," Aries waved her hand in his face to let him know how little she cared about his surfboard or what he thought of it. "They need a place to stay, and I ... well, we ... need them. It'll be good all around."

She turned and was marching off down the street before he managed to fully comprehend what she had just said.

"What do you mean, we *need* them?" he hissed into her ear when he finally managed to catch up with her.

With an annoyed expression on her face, she stopped a few yards shy of the bus and turned to him. "Tell me something. Just how rich are you, anyway?"

"Rich? Whoever said I was rich? I get some money every month, but apparently not as much as you think I do. If I watch it I can get along from month to month, but I sure as hell can't support every hippie we come across. And, if you haven't already figured it out, you are included with all the other street people you seem so intent on picking up."

"Hey, we need to get one thing straight. I'm no street person. I'm the girl who's going to get you everything you ever dreamed of - the best hash, some really super LSD, even peyote, if you're interested, and the best damned sex you'll ever have - and I'll do it without using up all your money. Now, if those things interest you, I suggest you just step aside and follow my lead."

Without bothering to look for his reaction, she yanked the front passenger door of the VW open and stepped in. The other girls followed her directions and found their places behind her.

Eddy stood beside the vehicle for a moment, lost in thought. Finally, without uttering another word, he climbed into the driver's seat and turned on the engine.

"Go to the first light and turn left," Aries directed from her place beside him. The firm tone of her voice gave little doubt as to who was in charge.

Chapter 11

ARIES

Aries didn't have an actual plan yet, but she was pretty sure she was on the right track. She smiled when the term 'Sisterhood of the Zodiac' popped into her mind. It had a certain ring to it. Counting herself, she already had three of the Zodiac signs - actually four, if she included Eddy. But including him in her little gang of astrologically named followers probably wasn't going to happen.

Oh, she planned on keeping him around, just not as part of the 'Sisterhood.' There were a dozen good reasons why holding onto a guy like him was a good idea. There was the sex thing, of course. He wasn't the best lay she'd ever had, but he wasn't the worst either. By the time she got all of her girls signed up, there would be twelve females to the one guy. She would need him, and maybe one or two more guys, to keep all of those women happy.

Plus, he did have that monthly paycheck coming in. She didn't know how much he got but it must be all right. Even though he drove a stupid beat up old VW, he always seemed to have enough money to buy food and pot. She figured she'd keep him around for the money, at least until it ran out.

It was also good to have a man around to fix things. So far he hadn't seemed much like a handy man, but there hadn't been anything for him to fix yet, either. He ought to be good for heavy lifting, if not for anything else.

"Hey, pull over," she suddenly ordered. They had only traveled a couple of miles away from the Haight so they were still deep in the maze of San Francisco's streets. "I need to make a phone call. There's a phone in that liquor store."

Without questioning her, Eddy pulled into the nearest parking space.

Good boy, Aries thought to herself. *He's getting trained even faster than I thought he would.* Still not as sure of him as she'd have liked, she grabbed the keys to the bus and took them with her as she entered the store.

The phone was answered on the eighth ring. She hadn't realized she'd been holding her breath until she heard the voice on the other end of the line.

"Hey, I need a place to stay." She didn't bother stating who she was. There was no way the guy she had called would forget her voice.

"Yeah, Aries ... Um, you know, like this isn't a good time for me."

"Yeah, dickhead, like I don't recall asking if it was good or not. I'll be there in fifteen minutes. That should be enough time for you to make it a good time."

When she got back to the bus she gave Eddy directions that took them to the south of the Market District by a circuitous route. It took Eddy ten minutes to realize they had passed the same street corner three times. He started to ask her where the hell she was taking them, but one look at her determined expression made him keep his thoughts to himself. The fact that she was apparently trying to get him so confused he'd never be able to find his way around San Francisco on his own rankled him a bit, but not enough to challenge her on it.

Oh yeah, he's getting better all the time, she thought as she fought to keep herself from smiling. He was going to be even easier to handle than she had hoped.

After wandering around the Market District for what seemed forever, Eddy found himself driving over the Bay Bridge, the bridge that connected San Francisco to the city of Oakland. After crossing its span, she directed him to Broadway, heading toward the port. Two blocks after they had passed the police headquarters she directed him to make a left hand turn. Now they were passing rows of dilapidated old warehouses, some of them in use, others noticeably abandoned.

"Okay, Eddy, you can park it right over there."

"Oh, I'm Eddy now, huh? When did you decide to call me by my real name instead of my sign, like you're doing with those two in the back seat?" His voice was petulant like he wouldn't be happy with any name she called him.

77

She wanted to laugh. He'd learn soon enough that she didn't give a flying flip if she'd hurt his little feelings. She'd call him whatever she damn well wanted to.

"Leo doesn't suit you, Eddy. Leos are lions, kings of the jungle and all that shit. You're no king, buddy. You're nothing but a little pussy cat."

If he got her full meaning of what she was calling him, he failed to show it. Yeah, he was a pussy, alright.

"Come on everyone, bring your stuff and get out. We're going to be here for a while."

Without bothering to see if her directions were being followed, she marched toward the side entrance to one of the most dilapidated warehouses on the street. It wasn't until she opened the door and stepped into the building that she stopped to see if the others were doing as she told them. It was with a sense of satisfaction mixed with disgust that she saw that all three were doing exactly as she had instructed. They were all such sheep!

The building smelled of mold and animal feces. Grime-covered windows let in less than half of the sun's intensity. It was one huge room which had apparently been used for storage. Here and there empty boxes, tattered blankets and various other clutter gave evidence that, although the building had been abandoned, it was not empty of human habitation.

Aries ignored everything on the ground floor as she found a set of stairs and began to ascend. Not bothering to knock, she opened the door at the head of the stairs. Up here there were separate rooms that had apparently been offices. Smaller rooms opened off from a center hallway that ran from one end of the building to the other.

She walked down to the end of the hallway to a space which had apparently been used as a communal area. This was where the bathrooms were located. Off to the right was an area that had served as a lunchroom, complete with cupboards and a sink. Someone had put a hot plate and a coffee pot on the counter, which could have used a good cleaning

In the right hand corner was a room that was at least twice as large as any of the others they had passed. It was this room Aries approached. Without bothering to knock she flung the door open and entered. It was the kind of place that would one day be converted to an expensive loft apartment but was now little more than a place where the homeless crashed.

Scattered about were bits and pieces of beat-up old furniture that had obviously been rescued from trash bins. To call the furnishings shabby would be kind, yet they somehow managed to make the place look like somebody's home. The wall facing Aries as she walked into the room was made up of floor-to-ceiling windows, from one end to the other. The other three walls were of red brick. Overhead were huge beams and air vents. The salvaged furniture had been arranged in the middle of the room facing the windows. The arrangement gave the place the feeling that someone had tried to do some interior decorating. Unfortunately, the view from the windows of nothing but another of the old warehouses managed to nullify the effort.

Sitting on a sagging old sofa was a man of uncertain age and nationality. Aries waited until everyone had entered the room before saying, "This is Richie, otherwise known as Spider. Spider, meet Libra and Aquarius. And, this guy over here, he's Eddy."

She made the introductions in an offhand manner, as if none of them was of much concern to her. "Spider's going to let us crash here for a few days."

She ignored the dark expression in Eddy's eyes as she continued giving instructions.

"Spider, find an empty office for the girls not too far from this room. I don't want them to get to feeling lonely." She also did not want them far enough from her to give them the idea of taking off. She wasn't about to start from scratch again. They were just too perfect for what she had in mind.

"My friend here," she nodded toward Eddy, "and I will take your mattress. It ought to be big enough for the two of us."

"Now, just a minute ..." Spider interjected.

"You," she jabbed her finger in his face, "can either put another mattress there in the corner, or find yourself another room.

"We're only going to be here for a few days." She let her voice settle back to its normal gravelly pitch. "You want to give a little hospitality to an old friend, right?"

"Yeah, sure, Aries. You do what you want."

Spider looked like a man who had given up on life long ago. Every garment he wore, from his knit cap to his threadbare socks, looked like they might have been worn by several others before he had found them.

His scraggly beard and tangled mass of greasy hair were streaked with gray. Actually, everything about him seemed gray. His clothes were all so faded it was impossible to tell what color they had once been. Even his skin was gray. And his eyes, while not being gray, were so dull it was impossible to tell what color they once were.

After she'd gotten everyone settled in their rooms, Aries had Eddy give Spider some money for a food run. She would have gone herself but she still wasn't sure enough of her little gang to leave them by themselves. Eddy was a loose cannon. And the girls? Well, the girls needed a bit of training, but she had a gut level feeling it wouldn't take long to make them hers forever.

Chapter 12

That first night, just after dusk, she instructed Spider to take Eddy down to the Haight while she took Libra and Aquarius out in the bus. The three women drove back across the Bay Bridge, heading into one of the city's seedier neighborhoods.

"Have either of you ever been out on the street before?" she asked as she began to slow down

"You mean like on the street to panhandle, or to hustle?" Libra asked.

"Either one. But what I was really wondering was if you had done any hustling."

"I've done a little," Aquarius said, her voice barely above a whisper.

"I'm no pro, but I've turned a trick two," Libra mumbled.

"What we need, girls, is money. If we're going to stick together, we've got to show Eddy we can hold up our end of the deal. He has money, but not nearly enough for what I'm planning."

Libra, who had taken the front passenger seat, turned wide eyes on her benefactor. "What kind'a plans are you talking about?"

Aries heard fear in the girl's voice, fear laced with hope. "I'm looking at making us a family, a family of girls just like us."

She had to suppress a smile at the word 'us.' She was nothing like these two hopeless pieces of shit, but if she was going to earn their loyalty, she had to make them believe it was 'all for one and one for all.'

"We need to stay at Spider's for a few days while we build up our cash reserve. The best way I can think of doing that is if you both do your part. Hell, I'll even turn a trick or two. It's not like I'm you're pimp, or anything. We're all in this together, right?"

The girl's assents were mumbled, indicating less than their total enthusiasm, but neither actually objected.

Aries drove around for a short time until she saw what she was looking for. She pulled over and parked outside a liquor store. All up and down the street were bars whose patrons were for the most part down-on-their-luck guys out looking for the most satisfaction they could get for the least amount of money. A couple of hookers were standing on one corner, but there seemed to be plenty of room for a few more.

"What we want is to hit the guys who come out of the bars before they get to their cars. We'll work together tonight, offer to give the creeps a party they won't forget, then get them into the bus. We can take them back to our place, use the mattress in your room. When we're finished, we'll bring 'em back here."

It wasn't the most brilliant plan, but it worked. In the time between dusk and when the bars closed the three women earned nearly five hundred dollars. Aries figured that at that rate she could pick up a couple more girls and be out of San Francisco in less than a week's time.

San Francisco was not her favorite town. In fact, after her last run-in with the law there, she had vowed to never step foot in it again. She knew more than a few cops in the City who would be very happy to see her behind bars.

Her last run-in, the time she had been arrested with nearly a pound of hash on her, was bad, really bad. She'd probably still be in jail if the dumb pig who arrested her hadn't been so willing to 'allow' her to give him a blow job in the back seat of his squad car.

She had no doubt he would have still hauled her off to jail, even with the sex. What saved her that night was the fact that she possessed a very low gag tolerance. The arrest happened not long after she had gorged herself on spaghetti and meat balls. It seemed the cop was more interested in cleaning himself off than keeping an eye on her. She was still laughing hysterically as she ran into the safety of the night.

During the day, when she was not escorting Libra and Aquarius on their nightly strolls, she was trolling the streets looking for the next two members of her little group. She took her time, rejecting girl after girl. The girls she was looking for had to have a certain look. They had to be reasonably good looking, but also desperate. She was looking for innocent-appearing girls who had been beat down by their unfulfilled dreams. She needed girls who needed her more than she needed them. Plus, they had to be the right sign.

That last requirement trumped all the others. She might look past one or two exceptions to her criteria, but they could not share an astronomical sign with any of the others. Each girl would be known only by her sign, with no duplications.

Aries had a very limited education, but what she lacked in formal schooling she made up for in street sense, and her street sense told her one thing: If you took away a person's personal vision of themselves, you could own them lock, stock and barrel. One easy way to do this was to take away the one thing they had possessed from the day they were born - their name. Take away their identity and replace it with one of your own choosing and you were one easy step toward total possession.

The Sisterhood of the Zodiac. Every time she thought of those words she felt a thrill of expectation. No names - just signs. When she was through grooming them, the girls of the Sisterhood would make the term 'Helter Skelter' fade into nothingness.

At one time she had held Charlie Manson up as an idol. He was the man! He was magic. But, after those murders she had come to see him in a different light. If he was such a big man, why had he sent women to do his work? The least he could have done would have been to go with them, to lead them into battle against the establishment. *He* should have drawn the first blood, damn it!

The Sisterhood of the Zodiac would be different. They would be Amazons, slashing and killing like wild animals. They would drink the blood of their victims, watch the last light of their lives fading from their eyes.

They would be goddesses!

Chapter 13

When they finally left the Bay Area, traveling north on Interstate Highway 5, the bus was filled to overflowing. Aries drove while Eddy sat in back with the two newest members of the group, Gemini and Cancer. If he'd had any reservations about where they might end up, they had gone up in smoke, an intense incense-smelling smoke, along with the sweet promise of lovemaking with the two nubile women who sat on either side of him on the seat behind the driver.

From the beginning of this journey, Aries had pictured Oregon as her destination. Now she wasn't so sure. Yes, she was still being drawn to the north, but somehow the thought of Oregon was slipping away. Something she had never experienced before was happening. The magnetic pull she was experiencing was so strong it felt as if it would draw her forward, even if she were to take her foot off the gas pedal.

The farther north she drove, the stronger the sensations building within her grew. With each passing mile she felt herself becoming more and more excited, an excitement tinged with fear, which only served to draw her further onward.

She did not question what was happening to her. Instead, she let the feelings sink deep within her, then expand until she thought she might explode with them. Any doubt she might have had about who she was and what she was preparing to do fell away, leaving her pure and open for the new woman she was becoming.

"We're hungry back here," Gemini whined from the back seat.

"Are we ever going to stop? I have to pee." This complaint came from Aquarius.

"There's a truck stop up the road a few miles," Cancer said, the one person in the vehicle who had traveled this road before. "Maybe we could stop for dinner and a potty break?"

Potty? Who the hell says 'potty,' Aries thought. *What have I got back there, a pack of grade schoolers?*

They had left the city of Redding behind and were climbing quickly along a tree-lined highway. All she could see on either side of the road were timber-covered mountains. She didn't need a map to tell her it might be a very long time before they reached another town.

What she really wanted to do was to go faster and faster, to catch up with whatever was pulling her toward it, but when she saw the off-ramp for the diner, she pulled off the highway. She hated to admit it but she was practically starving to death herself.

Feeling flush with the money the girls had earned doing tricks, Aries allowed everyone to choose whatever they wanted off the menu. She felt like celebrating, but for what she wasn't sure. All she knew was she was on the brink of something so far out she couldn't even imagine it.

Aries and Gemini were the only ones to order anything other than everyone else's usual extra-large hamburger, fries and shakes. Gemini's order of fried chicken and Aries' steak looked out of place on the same table as the fast food.

She didn't know why, but the fact that all of the others could not break out of their eating habits just this once stuck in Aries' craw. What was wrong with them, anyway? Didn't any of them, except for Gemini, have enough spunk to order something different?

"Where are you guys headed?" the waiter asked as he filled water glasses from an ice-filled pitcher.

"Oregon, eventually," Aries answered, "but right now we need to find a place to sleep that'll be big enough for all of us, yet not too expensive. Do you have any suggestions?"

"There're several motels coming up - some in Dunsmuir, the next city you'll come to - but I don't know if any of them have a place big enough for all you guys together. And, if they did, I'm bettin' it would cost a pretty penny. I do know of one place, though, but it might not be something you'd want to try."

"And why would that be?" Eddy asked.

"Well, it's the old mortuary up there in Dunsmuir. It's huge - has a whole bunch of rooms over the mortuary itself. It's been vacant since the last mortician's wife died in it. There's rumors the old place is haunted."

"Haunted!" Eddy laughed loud enough for patrons in the next room to crane their necks trying to see where all the noise was coming from. "What do they do, drag chains down the halls? Or maybe all they do is moan. Whatever, I don't think there's a ghost yet that was bad enough to scare *me* away."

"Like I said, that's the rumor. The one thing that makes me think there might be something to it is that when the old lady died she left the place to a friend of hers who refused to ever enter it. She's never sold it and, from what I hear, she doesn't want to have anything to do with it. So it's just sitting there, probably rotting away."

"Where is this old mortuary?" Aries asked. She couldn't hide her curiosity. "Are you sure nobody's living there?"

"Been empty for years. I figure the lady who owns it is afraid of the ghosts."

Aries' gaze never left the waiter as she imagine herself living in a genuine haunted mortuary. There was definitely something about the idea that appealed to her.

"I hear she says she'll never step foot in it again. Might be ripe for squatters, if they was to move in and just stay there."

"Can you do that?"

The man now had Aries full attention. A free house, big enough for all of the Sisterhood? Was it even possible?

"Sure can. I don't know all the specifics, bein' as I'm not a lawyer, but I've heard that all you have to do is move in, start getting your mail sent there and pay property taxes. After a while, I don't know how long, you can get full title."

As they walked back to the VW, Aries made up her mind. She was going to at least check the old place out. As far as getting title to it, well, that sounded like a bunch of garbage to her, but who knew? The way things were going for her since she'd latched onto Eddy, as far as she could see anything was possible. It was definitely worth checking out.

Part Three

Dunsmuir

Chapter 14

The citizens of the small city of Dunsmuir, CA, took little notice of the wildly painted VW bus that entered the environs of their city late that July night. Straddling Interstate 5, which stretched from the border of Mexico all the way to Alaska, the town was accustomed to seeing just about any vehicle humanity could dream up pass through. It was a town through which thousands of travelers passed each day, some stopping off for a meal or a night's rest, others passing it without giving it any more attention than a quick glance at its city limits sign.

It was true that the bulk of the hippie days were past, but it was still not unusual to see hold-outs of the life style come through town now and again. A few of Dunsmuir's citizens looked at the flower and rainbow painted vehicle with smiles, recalling the days when they themselves had been part of the movement. What good times those had been!

The morning after the Sisterhood of the Zodiac arrived in town, Jeff Withers noticed their bus parked at the local grocery store. Forgetting for the moment what had brought him to the store, he circled the vehicle, letting his fingers rest here and there on flowers that had obviously been painted by a less than talented hand. In that moment he was nowhere near the city in the mountains. Instead, he felt himself transmitted to the streets of San Francisco. His naturally curly black hair was long and wild. He was proud that he was the only white man he knew who could tease his hair into a style that rivaled even the wildest black man's 'fro. He wore blue and white striped hip huggers, held up by a macramé belt. Over his long-sleeved Gypsy-styled shirt he wore a buck skin vest with fringe that hung almost to his knees.

My God, there had never been a time like that! The marches, the women and the smokes. And, oh, the music! He was convinced there never had been, nor would there ever be, a time of better music. He was most likely right about that.

Nor would there ever be a time when a person's political beliefs were more important. He had been part of a movement that might actually have stopped a war! He'd gloried in the jeers and threats of the Establishment. He had felt the blows from the pigs' nightsticks. The two scars that marred his face had been given to him during one of his arrests for marching peacefully against the Vietnam War. They forever marked him as a man who lived true to his beliefs during a time when the truth was treated with disrespect and fear. Yeah, those were the days, all right. But those days had been over for him for a long time now.

The film of nostalgia gone from his eyes, Jeff Withers turned his back on the vehicle and his memories. Wearing a bemused smile, he entered the grocery store as he pulled Marie's shopping list out of his pocket.

Reaching for a shopping cart, his attention was drawn to the couple who had just finished checking out. He was a tall, blond surfer type of guy. His female companion wore the clothes and hairstyle of a hippie chick. Although they were obviously together, they sure as hell didn't look like they were a couple. He had little doubt but that the VW belonged to one of them but he couldn't help but wonder which one's name was on the pink slip. The guy sure didn't have the look of a hippie, but the girl didn't look like she had ever had enough bread in her pocket to pay for any vehicle, even one as old and beat-up as the one parked outside.

The door closed behind the strangers as Jeff began to fill his shopping basket with items from his wife's list. Living along the I-5 corridor as he did, with people getting off the highway just long enough to get a bite to eat or to fill up on gas, he doubted he'd ever see those two again.

Chapter 15

Aries couldn't believe her luck. When they arrived at Dunsmuir the night before she'd been too tired to give much attention to the old building the waiter had directed them to. All she knew was it was really big and kind'a spooky. And, of course, it was as dark as a witch's heart once they got inside. Resolving to get the electricity hooked up the next day, she was relieved to find that the water had not been turned off. Barking orders as she went, she managed to get everyone out of the van and asleep on the floor of the first floor level. One of the girls started whining about not wanting to sleep with nothing more than light blankets over her, but Aries shut her up before her complaints gave the others any ideas of not following her orders.

After getting a fairly good night's sleep, she began to explore the old place. And what a place it was. The room where they had all slept the previous night was absolutely huge. She surmised it might have been where funerals were once held. It was interesting, the way it had been designed so that it could be divided into two rooms by closing it off with panels that slid back into the walls when they were not being used.

Her nose wrinkled with distaste as her gaze took in the overly ornate old-timey furniture. The stuff was probably worth a lot of money, but she was going to have to get rid of it. She smiled when she realized that, even though she didn't like the furnishings, they would serve her purpose very well when she sold them off.

She didn't have to close her eyes to imagine how the room would look when she finished decorating it. After she'd gotten rid of those hideous drapes, she would replace them with a rainbow of Indian saris. The bare hardwood floors were just begging for some oriental rugs and pillows.

She'd have to keep the two Victorian sofas, at least for a little while - not everyone liked sitting on the floor all the time - but as soon as she found some good old beat-up couches, they'd go the way as all the other furniture. It was the seventies, for God's sake, not the turn of the last century.

Standing in the middle of the room, she closed her eyes and let herself savor the way it would be when she finished redecorating. The room would be filled with color, the lyrical sounds of a sitar, the scent of incense and some really good weed. A smile slowly crept over her face. This room was where she would capture the souls of the Sisterhood.

She opened her eyes. It was time to get to work. She had to get everything up and running smoothly, then get back to the City where she could find everything she needed to turn this place into what she needed it to be - a place where she could mold the minds and souls of her followers.

With a nod of acceptance of her vision, she returned to what needed to be done first - finishing the inspection of the building she intended to call home until she had accomplished her life's mission, which was to make the name 'Charlie Manson' nothing more than a blip on the history of monsters, the little weasel-faced creep. Charlie Manson? When she was finished, no one would even remember his name.

She soon discovered that inspecting the entire building was going to take a while. She could not have imagined she'd one day live in a house with three whole stories of living space, not counting the basement, where the day to day mortician's work had been accomplished.

The place wasn't just a mortuary - it was a God-damned mansion! And, from what she'd seen so far, every single room was furnished. The guy at the diner hadn't mentioned that. She'd figured they'd be hitting the local thrift shops for mattresses; what she hadn't even dreamed was that they would each have a room to themselves.

That was, of course, until she had filled-out the ranks of the Zodiac. When she had, they would just have to get used to sharing. Everyone, except herself, of course.

"Hey! We're hungry down here," Libra's whiny voice reached her from the floor below. "When are we going out to eat?"

* * *

Libra was still whining when Aries and Eddy returned from shopping. "I don't see why we can't go out for breakfast. I don't like just everything. That's why I like going out.

"Well, I'm real sorry about that." Aries' voice dripped with sarcasm. "But, unless you have a bank full of money in that backpack of yours, that's not going to happen. We're cooking for ourselves, and that's that!"

"Cook? Who's going to cook? How'll we know if they're any good? Like I said, there's a lot of stuff I don't like."

"Then I guess you'll just have to become our little chef, Libra," Aries answered. "I like scrambled eggs, not too dry, and my bacon crisp. And don't burn the toast!" were her last words as she turned her back on the very astonished girl.

"What the f ...?"

"Oh, and don't bother asking the others what they want. What I want is what everyone else gets. The kitchen's through that door, in case you haven't already found it. You better get started. It's getting late."

Aries didn't wait around to see what Libra's reaction would be to having been treated like a servant. She already knew. She hadn't come up with the idea of picking her girls according to their birth signs for nothing. If there was one thing she considered herself to be an expert on, it was the Zodiac. She knew each sign's strengths and weaknesses. Or, at least she thought she did.

Right at that moment the only thing she wanted to do was to finish her inspection of the house. There was one room she hadn't checked out yet besides the basement. It was the room on the second floor at the end of the stairs.

From the moment she'd stepped onto the second floor earlier in the day she had been drawn to that one particular room. It was as if a magnetic power drew her to it. But, instead of responding to its energy, she forced herself to inspect every other living space of the building first. She instinctively knew there was something special hidden behind the door to that room which was meant for her eyes only. Something so extraordinary it promised, or threatened, to change her life forever.

Much like a parent might make a child wait for a special treat, she had forced herself to turn away from the room and continue with her inspection of the rest of the building. A quick inspection of the other rooms would answer all the questions she might have about them. The same could not be said about the room she called to her. When she finally did step across the threshold to that room she might not want to ever step back out.

Now, as she mounted the stairs one slow step at a time, her curiosity began to build. What was there about that one particular room that made it different from the rest of the building? Did everyone feel its power, or was it just meant for her?

As she took her first step into the hallway that led to the room, she felt curiosity change to expectation, then expectation change to a sense of destiny. As she opened the door and stepped into the room, all of the other emotions abruptly morphed into utter exhilaration. She took one step farther into the room and stopped. Standing perfectly still she let her gaze drift slowly around the space, taking in the full spectrum of her surroundings. Her heart began to race. Her breath came in short bursts. Her lips were drawn into a smile of pure satisfaction. She was embraced with an almost overwhelming sense of welcoming. She knew instinctively that she was home at last.

In the farthest corner was a four poster bed made of a dark wood. It was a very masculine piece, completely devoid of the scrolls and fancy turns so familiar to the Victorian era. Aries was fascinated to note that, while all of the other beds in the house were all neatly made, this one looked as if it had not been touched since it was last slept in. A crazy quilt lay in a heap on the floor as if it had been thrown aside. The sheets and pillows were still on the bed in a tangled mess.

Her gaze did not waver from the pile of linens as she slowly approached the bed. Without questioning what she was doing, Aries climbed onto the bed and lay down on the sheets. As she pulled the rumpled linens over her, she let her eyes drift shut.

Taking in a deep breath, she took in the scent of the man who had once called the room his own. She wallowed in the nearness of a man she had never known; a man she would never know physically, yet she willingly offered her soul.

Driven by the need to know more about the man she was so eager to give herself to, Aries rose from the bed, walked over to the closet and opened it. Inside were his clothes. Very dated suits - all of them in dark, somber tones - and white starched dress shirts hung neatly, all ready to be worn at a moment's notice. A light coating of dust was all that marred the brilliantly polished surface of various styles of men's shoes that lined the bottom of the closet. On the top shelf were hats, all clearly from a long gone era.

Pulling one of the hats down, she placed it on her head. It fit perfectly, as if it had been made just for her. Reaching out her hand, she let her fingers roam over the suits and shirts, sensing the texture of the cloth, feeling … just exactly what was she feeling?

She was drawn to the scent and the feel of the contents of the closet. Gently pushing shoes aside, she stepped in amongst the suits, wrapping the sleeves of one of the jackets around her as if the man it had once belonged to was holding her in his arms. Allowing herself to be lost in the sensation of the cloth against her skin, she drew in a deep breath, as if by doing so she could take in the spirit of the man to whom the clothes had once belonged deep within herself.

In this room she felt welcomed like no other place she had ever known. She felt an intense sense of homecoming sweep over her, holding her in a tight embrace, as if it would never let her go. Without questioning what she was doing, or what the consequences of her actions might be, she opened herself to the sensation, letting the warmth of possession clasp her tightly.

Chapter 16

Each time Aries entered the room her heightened sense of awareness seemed greater than before. Each morning she rose from his bed she felt closer to the man who had once worn the garments that hung in the closet.

In the night he came to her, showing her his face. "I am Horace," he whispered to her in her dreams. "You are mine, and I am yours." His kisses were roughly possessive. The strength of his arms told her he would never let her go - not that she wanted him to.

She knew his name and what he looked like, but very little else. But that didn't bother her. She knew what was important: that although he had been gone from this world for a very long time, his essence still lived within the walls of the room; and, yes, within her as well.

He came to her in many ways. It was in her sleep that he told her his name and first let her see him. In the beginning, except for the charged atmosphere of the room, that was all he allowed her. She yearned for more, yet knew she must not ask. She cherished every moment he shared with her, every insight into his being. But there was more to him, she knew in her gut there was. Would he ever give her all she desired of him?

Gradually, as she learned how to put her own desires and expectations aside, he came to her visually more and more often. Until all she had to do was step into the room and call his name, and he would be there. She never considered that she was calling him in the way that someone would demand the presence of another. She was his servant, not the other way around.

But she was a very willing servant. By following his orders her own strength grew exponentially. It was such a powerful sensation to sit in the center of the circle he had directed her to draw on the floor and to let him fill her with his energy. She would sit on the floor, her ankles crossed close to her body, her back straight, her head erect. She would place her hands on her folded knees palms-up and close her eyes. One by one she would open her chakras to him and beseech him to enter her. Starting at the top of her head, she let him pour himself into her. She welcomed his knowledge as it flowed in through her third eye. Step-by-step down the path of her body, he came to her until he reached the very core of her - her root chakra.

The first time she reached a climax as he came to her through her root she was pleasantly shocked. It certainly hadn't been anything she had expected or even imagined. The flow of his energy filling her entire body had been breathtaking enough to satisfy even her most erotic dreams. How could she ever repay him for such a gift?

She quickly became addicted to his ministrations. If she hadn't worried that he might tire of satisfying her if she came to him too often, she would have found herself sitting in the circle every minute of every day. Instead, she saved their times together for her first waking moments and for just before she crawled into his bed.

During the time between morning and night Aries busied herself by following his orders. She did not know his exact plan for The Sisterhood, but knew the strength of her leadership was essential for its success. It was an overwhelming responsibility that she realized had been thrust upon her long before she had come to the house. It was he who had placed her outside the diner the day Eddy found her. And, although she had fought it, it was because of Horace that she had gone with Eddy to San Francisco. How else could she have found Aquarius and Libra? For that matter, how else would she have known to follow the Zodiac in picking out the women who would one day also be his followers? None of it would have happened had it not been for Horace's influence. Her was her All - always had been and always would be. Through him she would live forever, if not on the face of this earth then in the world of infamy.

Chapter 17

Looking back at the first few weeks of the Sisterhood's life in Dunsmuir, Aries was pleased with all she had accomplished. The mixed bag of strangers who had joined together to journey to Dunsmuir had taken on the semblance of a family.

By using Eddy's meager credit status, Aries managed to get the electricity turned on at the mansion. Intent upon obtaining the property through Squatter's Rights if it was possible, she went to City Hall and requested the bills for services be sent to the property address under her name. She wasn't entirely sure there was such a thing as legal Squatter's Rights, but if there was she was not going to lose any time getting herself established as a permanent resident at the address.

For the most part, Eddy was content to let Aries handle all the details of daily life as long as he was fed fairly decent food, had enough weed to smoke and was kept entertained by one or more of the girls. Following Aries' instructions, the girls tried to keep him happy without allowing him to favor one over the other. Sometimes he felt as if he had been transported into a harem of young, nubile women whose only purpose was to serve his every need. He rarely complained.

He was only too pleased to accept Aries' decision that he should occupy the apartment at the top of the mansion. It wasn't exactly a bachelor's pad, but it was private and roomy enough for his needs. He almost balked at her decision when he first opened the closet in the one-bedroom apartment and found it filled with what could only be described as old ladies' clothing. But after Libra and Aquarius cleaned the place up and emptied the closet, he decided he could be quite happy there.

And he *was* happy, enjoying sweet lovemaking, relaxing smokes and good food for all of two weeks, before Aries told him that as the 'man of the house' he needed to get a job. Yes, he did have that monthly check from his trust fund coming in, but it would only go so far, especially now that the family had grown to six, and would soon consist of even more.

Trying to figure out just what kind of work he was most suitable for proved to be more than a little difficult. His resume was pitifully short. He had been a student ... but not a very good one. He had helped out at the Spahn Ranch ... but hadn't done anything that would suit him for a job in the small mountain town in which they were now living. His only true skill was as a surfer, but that was not about to earn him much money with him living so far from the ocean. In truth, Eddy was not suited for any type of work that took skill or training.

He eventually managed to land a dishwashing job at one of the local restaurants. If he ever noticed how far he had fallen from the dreams his parents had once had for him, he never mentioned it.

He actually liked working at the restaurant. He enjoyed the companionship of his coworkers and was not challenged to do more with his life than to go through each day with as little conflict as possible.

And when, after they had been living in the mortuary for only a few days, he had been all but banished from the lower rooms of the building, he had barely given it a thought. Sometimes the accumulative noise of all those women's voices got on his nerves. Indeed, he was more than pleased when Aries suggested that if he would agree to stay in his own apartment she would see that he was never at a loss for food, weed or female companionship. All he'd ever have to do would be to continue contributing to the kitty and all of his needs would be taken care of to his complete satisfaction. It sounded like a sweet deal to him.

Libra and Aquarius teamed up and took over all of the cooking and cleaning at the mansion. Until she had come to Dunsmuir Libra had barely known what was in a kitchen, but her friend Aquarius was the oldest child in a family of twelve children whose drunken father had abandoned his wife soon after the birth of their last child. Aquarius' mother had been forced to hold down two jobs, leaving the raising of the children to her oldest daughter. What Aquarius did not know about epicurean delights she made up for with a practical approach to

111

food. No one starved at the mortuary, even if the food tended to consist of very simple fare.

Gemini, one of the newest women to join the group, found a job in Mt. Shasta, the town about ten miles north of Dunsmuir, working as a housekeeper at one of the larger motels. She didn't bring in much money, but in a small town like Dunsmuir you sometimes had to take work you wouldn't normally consider in more financially vibrant communities.

The other new girl, Cancer, had actually worked at a bank before deciding to leave her husband and seek a life of adventure out on the West Coast. Known by her former name, Syble Miller, to her new employer, she went back to keeping banker's hours. Although the job reminded her of one of the reasons why she had run away from her past life, knowing she had the Sisterhood waiting for her back at the mortuary at the end of each work day managed to keep her on the job and drawing a steady paycheck.

Although their various jobs kept the women busy during the day, their evenings were what helped to mold them into what eventually became a living, breathing inhuman organism. Each day, after dinner was finished and the kitchen cleanup complete, every female member of the mortuary's residents gathered together in the redecorated living room. Candles burned on the mantel and throughout the entire room, giving the room a subdued atmosphere. Ravi Shankar's sitar music played in the background, blending lightly with the tone of women's voices. The women, relieved from the need to wear clothing appropriate to their specific working conditions, lounged around the room in loose fitting garments.

As the hours passed, fumes from the continuous smoking of marijuana spread throughout the room until it reached a density thick enough to make someone not purposely participating in the drug to become light-headed. It was then that the conversation became the most intense.

"You know who you guys make me think of?" Aries asked one night. She was answered only with dull stares from a couple of the Sisters. "You make me think of the Manson family, that's who." She gave them the answer even though no one had actually asked. "They were good, the whole lot of them, except for that rat, Charlie."

"Hey, Charlie was the king, man! If it wasn't for him no one would have ever heard of the others." Cancer was sitting up now, looking as if she was ready for a fight.

"No, no, no," Aries replied, waving the hand that was holding her joint at the woman as if by doing so she would make Cancer's words go away, "Charlie's nothing! Those girls, they were the ones who went out and showed the pigs what they were made of. If it wasn't for them, nobody would have ever heard of Charlie."

"But Charlie was the one who decided who got offed."

"If he's so great, why did he send the family out to do his business? You didn't see him getting blood on his hands."

"But without Charlie, there wouldn't have been a Manson family."

"Yeah, maybe so, but there still would have been the girls, they'd a just been called something else. Hell, for all we know, they might have gotten rid of a lot more pig lovers if they'd been the ones doing the planning."

Silence settled over the room as each girl either gave more thought to the subject or merely relaxed back into her drug-induced stupor.

"I think we ought to show good ol' Charlie what a bunch of real women can do without a sorry ass like him. Fuck, a Sisterhood like ours could make the Manson family look like a bunch of losers."

Aries leaned back into the depths of her huge pillow, allowing her head to tip so far back she was staring up at the ceiling. Now and again she took a languid drag on her joint.

She said no more about Charlie Manson or his family that night. She remained content that the seed she had planted into her followers' minds would flourish as time wore on. There was no timetable for what she had in mind, but when the time was right she intended to have each and every one of the Sisters there to back her up in an act so infamous all of their names would be known forever.

Chapter 18

Horace revealed to her the morning after she first brought up Charlie Manson's name that it was time for her to take the next step. It was during their early morning special time together, the time of day when no one else dared bother her. It was the time when his presence was all she needed or wanted. He told it to her just before giving her the most devastatingly fabulous orgasm of her life.

"Bring them to me," he had said. "Do it tonight." And then he told her in exquisite detail what she must do and what she must say. And to whom these things were to be done.

Aries left the house soon after breakfast that morning without telling anyone where she was going or when she would be back. Following Horace's directions, she pointed the old VW bus north on I-5. She never questioned how he knew where she would find the articles needed for the night's events. It was enough that he had placed the image of a skull with the top of its head removed into her mind that morning, along with explicit directions of where she would find such an item. She drove north, crossing the Oregon border. She continued until her instincts told her to leave the highway and head west. She took turn after turn, never questioning her choices, until she reached an old building that looked as if it might collapse at any moment.

She entered without knocking, knowing in her heart she was expected.

An old woman sat behind a grime-covered showcase. "It's about time you got here," the old crone complained.

Aries knew she was not expected to speak.

"I've got them here," the woman continued as she reached down to a box that sat at her feet.

Aries gave the woman the amount of money Horace had dictated she take with her, then took the box to the bus. She did not speak one word to the old woman throughout the entire transaction. She made no more stops on her way back to the mortuary. She did not open the box until she was back in her room, the door securely locked behind her.

Placing the box on top of Horace's old dresser, she withdrew the contents, one precious piece at a time. Her fingers tingled with excitement as she held each glass skull in the palm of her hand. They were perfect replicas of the human skull, with only one difference: The crown of each skull was missing, turning them into the perfect containers to hold the tribute Horace demanded.

She lined them up along the dresser, all twelve of them, from her left to her right. Behind each skull she placed a red candle. When she was finished, Aries stepped back and gazed at the altar she had constructed. She prayed he would be pleased.

* * *

The stroke of mid-night was marked by a light tapping on Aries' door. Her heartbeat quickened as she crossed the room. This was it, the beginning. This night's work was crucial to the plan. If it did not go as Horace directed, there would be no true Sisterhood of the Zodiac. And, if there was no Sisterhood, Horace would have little need for her.

Aries opened the door, praying that both girls had accepted her invitation. She drew in a quick breath of relief at the sight of both Aquarius and Libra standing before her. She stood still for a moment, allowing the glowing candles of the room's altar to silhouette her figure. Without saying a word, she dipped her head in greeting, then stepped aside, gesturing with her right hand that they were to enter.

The light from the candles was barely enough for the girls to see the names of all of the Zodiac signs painted on the outside rim of the circle Aires had drawn on the floor.

Still remaining silent, she pointed each girl toward her Zodiac name. Stepping over to her own, she sat down, facing toward the center of the circle. Following her lead, each of the young women found their places. At Aries' place, just inside the circle was one of the glass skulls. Inside of the skull was a small amount of a dark red substance. Inside the circle, was the symbol of Aries' Zodiac sign, drawn in what appeared to be blood.

Aries bent her knees and brought her feet close, crossing her ankles. Laying her hands upon her knees, palms facing upward, she sat quietly, eyes closed, as she drew in and expelled three deep breaths. The others, believing that what they had been asked to participate in must be some sort of ritual, followed their leader's example.

Aries' mind raced with uncertainty. The next words she spoke might be the most important she would ever utter. She couldn't help worrying that she might be inadequate to the task. *Please, Horace, help me! Give me the words and I will say them. I am but your humble servant. My only wish is to do your bidding.*

A sense of calmness and warmth slipped over her, starting from the crown of her head, then traveling downward until it embraced every inch of her body. He was with her. Her words would be his words. She had nothing to fear.

"Welcome to my sanctuary, my sisters," she said in greeting. "I thank you for accepting my invitation. The invitation I offered you is what brought you here tonight. But the invitation I will offer each of you tonight will bring you something far better than my mere presence. It will bring you one step closer to a glory far beyond your wildest imagination. It will bring you a magnificence that most people are too weak to even dream of.

It will give you the strength and inspiration to accomplish your own personal absolute. " These things will come to you only if you accept them with your total being. This is an offer I make this night to only the two of you. Because you were the first to accept my offer of sanctuary, you are being offered the glorious opportunity to be the first to join me as full members in the Sisterhood of the Zodiac. "Now, tell me, Libra, will you accept my invitation?

"I ... I will, Aries. You know I will do whatever you ask of me."

"And you, Aquarius, will you accept my invitation?"

"I will, Aries. I am honored to be asked."

Aries fought off the temptation to let out a huge sigh of relief. If the Sisterhood was to do Horace's work she must never let the members see her in even one moment of weakness.

"Very well, then, so it shall be." She closed her eyes and spread her arms wide in a gesture of blessing. "Welcome, my sisters."

The two girls exchanged curious glances as they bent their heads in acceptance of her blessing.

"It is time now for you to make an offering to the Sisterhood." Once again the two girls glanced at one another. What could either of them offer?

"Don't worry, my children. The Sisterhood takes nothing from its own, nothing but your loyalty and devotion. The Sisterhood takes only from outside the ring of the Zodiac. The

119

offerings it wishes will come from non-believers. "You must go into the night to find your offerings. Go into the temples of others and take the meaningless symbols of their wealth."

"You want us to steal things out of churches?" Libra's eyes reflected her shock.

"If that is what you see as others' temples, yes. But not everyone sees a church as their temple. Many see their own homes as their temples, their own possessions. "Now, go, my sisters. When this task is complete, you will be one step closer to being full members of the Sisterhood, and one step closer to being placed in your proper order of authority."

Chapter 19

Aries had difficulty sleeping that night. Her mind raced with excitement after having completed the first Sacred Circle with Libra and Aquarius. Horace had been pleased with how she had handled it. The ritual, the sacred words, they had all come from him. But, as his most loyal follower, they had come through her. She had done well. She knew this because he had not only told her so, he had shown her by giving her the most intense loving experience yet after the girls left.

Usually she would have fallen fast asleep within minutes of putting her head on her pillow after receiving Horace's special attention, but not that night. While she was still in the throes of passion he had whispered new instructions into her ear. He was pleased with what she had accomplished so far, but now was not the time to sit back and gloat. At first light he expected her to be heading south on I-5, on her way to taking the next step toward his ultimate goal.

After little more than three hours of sleep, Aries was up meeting one more time with her lover even before the sun had begun to crest the mountains to the east. She needed his guidance and his affection, both of which she received in full.

It was still dark as she went down to the main floor of the building and began her search. He hadn't shown her what she was to take with her, but she knew she would recognize each item when she saw them.

As soon as she stepped into the large room that had once held services for the dead her gaze was pulled to the painting that hung directly over the fireplace. It was a landscape, one that had held very little attraction to her before. It was so … so nice, so peaceful, it nearly made her gag. Yet now, as she gazed up at it, she realized it was obviously an original oil and it might be worth a great deal of money. Walking closer, she tried to read the name of the artist, but could make nothing of the odd scribble.

With a shrug of her shoulders, she reached up for it. It didn't matter what she thought of it. If Horace wanted her to take it with her, she would not question it. Everything he had told her so far, no matter how odd it seemed at the time, worked out perfectly. She was not about to question him now.

With the painting leaning on the wall beside the front door, she went back into the room to see what else she could find. Once again she was drawn to the fireplace, this time to the two silver flower vases that had flanked the painting. Taking one down from the mantle, she turned it upside down so she could read the words etched on the bottom. What she learned was that she was holding a Reid and Barton sterling silver period piece. What she knew about silver was absolutely nothing but it didn't take a genius to realize the silver alone in the thing might be worth a fortune. It was huge. At least 18 inches tall, it was heavy enough to sink a ship. And there were two of them.

After placing her treasures in the VW, she pointed the bus south and was nearly to Redding by the time she realized she was starving for breakfast.

She was halfway through her Denver omelet when she realized just how brilliant Horace truly was. He knew every single step she needed to make. If she had left any earlier she would have cruised right through the city without even thinking about stopping to purchase the clothing she would need to establish herself as a woman who might actually own the items she would be trying to sell. If she walked into a gallery, or even a pawn shop, wearing her hippie garb, the first thing the clerk would think was that she was a thief.

After paying the bill, she asked the waitress to direct her to the nearest department store. When she left the store the hippie clothes were in a shopping bag and she was wearing a pair of chocolate brown gabardine slacks, a cream colored long-sleeved silk blouse and brown and white spectator pumps.

If she'd had more time, she would have gone into the store's beauty shop for a shampoo and cut, but instead she combed her wild hair straight back from her brow and twisted its mass into a very sedate bun at the nape of her neck. After applying a peachy-toned lipstick to lips that had not seen a speck of makeup in years, she was certain she looked like a woman who might legitimately own a priceless piece of art and heirloom silver.

When she reached Sacramento she marched into the first art gallery on her list with a steady step and head held high. She was there to do business. When she walked out of the store her newly purchased handbag held five thousand dollars that had not been there before.

She wanted to laugh out loud, but didn't, of course. It would never do to let herself get too comfortable. She still had those two silver vases to unload.

She could hardly believe it. Five thousand dollars for that ugly old thing! And the crazy thing was she would bet every dollar in her purse it was worth a whole lot more. If she'd had any doubt that it was, when she told the store manager that she needed cash rather than a store check, he'd told her to stay right there while he ran to the bank. He hadn't been gone more than ten minutes when he came back with fifty one hundred dollar bills.

At her next stop she knew she'd been cheated when she walked out of the pawn store with only four hundred dollars more. What a creep that guy had been. He almost salivated when she pulled the first vase out of its wrapping and placed it on the counter. He knew exactly what she had, then had the gall to offer her a measly one hundred dollars for the pair. She'd talked him up to four hundred, but only after he'd agreed to toss in a beautiful little dagger that caught her eye.

Her first choice had been an even swap for a thirty-eight snub nosed revolver, but when the guy insisted that she fill out a form, show him her ID and then wait a few days before she could take it with her, she went ahead and took the money and the knife. There were other easier and cheaper ways to get a gun. *Cheaper?* Hell, why pay money when she could get her girls to get her one for free? All they had to do was find the right house to burglarize.

As she pulled out of the pawn shop's parking lot her stomach reminded her it was already two hours past lunch time. Damn, if she didn't get a move on, she wouldn't get back to Dunsmuir until the middle of the night. So far she'd only accomplished two of Horace's demands. She had the money, now she needed to find another girl to add to the Sisterhood. Lunch would just have to wait.

Chapter 20

NANCY

Nancy sat on a bench outside the Greyhound bus station smoking a cigarette she'd bummed off of an old man. The way the smoke seared her lungs told her that not only was it not her preferred brand, it was one of the cheapest ones on the market. She smoked slowly, trying to make the comfort it gave her last for as long as possible. When she lit up she made a bargain with herself: As long as it lasted she would remain where she was; when she was done she would get up and do something. She just wished she knew what the 'something' would be!

She glanced at the red glow at the end of the cigarette, measuring what was left of the tobacco with her eyes. Less than two inches. How many drags would it take to make those two inches disappear, she wondered. Five? Ten? If she took short puffs, could she make it last even longer?

Without being conscious of it, tears began sliding down her cheeks, trailing liquid mascara along with them, giving her the look of a bedraggled clown. People were coming and going all around her. Some gave her curious, furtive glances, others kept their eyes as far from her as possible. She didn't know who she hated the most, the people who saw her as someone to be pitied, or the ones who found her too repulsive to even acknowledge her presence. She drew more smoke into her lungs, this time not bothering to see what was left of the cigarette. No matter how much was there, it would never be enough.

"The hell with it," she muttered as she threw the butt to the asphalt and ground it out. She rose from the bench without giving a glance at the bus terminal, the building that had been her home for the past three nights.

No one had bothered her there as long as she had a couple of dollars to spend at the coffee counter, but now that the last of her babysitting money was gone she was nothing more than another bum. When she saw other vagrants being rousted from the benches where they slept, she made a quick exit from the station.

"You look like a young lady who could use a cup of coffee and maybe a bite to eat."

The woman's voice came from directly behind her. She was startled, yet too hungry to not at least turn to see who was speaking.

Nancy looked into the young woman's hazel brown eyes - eyes that were looking directly into her own.

"I ..." To her shame, fresh tears began pouring from her eyes.

"Hey, don't go crying on me," the woman said. Her smile was so warm, so accepting. "Come on, let's get the two of us something to eat. I can't remember ever being so hungry! How about you? Does a steak sound all right?"

Before she knew what was happening, Nancy found herself being helped into a wildly painted old VW bus. She was just getting settled when her benefactor climbed into the driver's side and pointed the vehicle away from the bus station. She didn't know whether to grateful or scared to death. What she did know, however, was that no matter what happened now she was just going to have to make the best of it. She had left her very last hope for salvation back there on that bus bench.

* * *

What she had feared might be a nightmare seemed to be turning out to be the best dream she'd ever had. Here she sat, facing this really nice lady, in the fanciest restaurant she'd ever been in, waiting to be served a sirloin steak, stuffed baked potato and creamed spinach. If this was heaven she was ready for it.

"Now that we're settled and everything, I think it's time we got acquainted with each other," the woman said, her warm smile making her words incredibly soothing. "My name is Aries," she said as she reached across the table to shake Nancy's hand. "And may I ask yours?"

Nancy started to take Aries hand, then drew hers back. She couldn't remember the last time she'd washed her hands. They must be filthy!

"Uh, my name's Nancy, and I … I need to use the lady's room," she mumbled. Scooting the chair back so fast it almost upended, she left the table. Her image in the bathroom mirror even more embarrassed than she'd been before. "Oh, my God," she moaned as she splashed water over her face.

Using the soap from the dispenser, she scrubbed her face, hands, arms, neck and everything else that was exposed until her skin turned pink. Wishing for a hot tub and a good long soak, she relieved herself in the toilet, washed her hands again and rejoined her new friend.

"Wonderful! You arrived just in time", Aries said with a smile. "I really do hate eating alone. Now, dig in."

Nancy did not have to be asked twice. She tore into the steak like she hadn't eaten a piece of meat for longer than she could remember. Actually, she had never eaten a steak as huge or as tender as the one she was now shoving into her mouth at record speed. Indeed, she reminded herself, in all of her sixteen years, she could remember only eating any kind of steak a couple of times.

She had finished the steak and was forking the first bite of sour cream-filled baked potato into her mouth when Aries asked, "If you don't mind my asking, Nancy, what's your sign?"

"My what?" she responded through a mouthful of food.

"You know, what's your astrological sign?"

Aries might have been speaking a foreign language as far as Nancy was concerned. Was the lady into astronomy?

"If you tell me your birth date I can tell you what sign of the Zodiac you were born under. You have heard of the Zodiac, haven't you?"

"Well, yeah … sure. I just never thought about it much, that's all. I was born on November the second."

"Great! Your sign is Scorpio, which is just perfect."

"How do you mean *perfect?*" She was eating slower now. No longer feeling as if she might pass out from hunger, she was allowing herself to savor the mixture of flavors of the potato and its dressings.

"I'm part of what you might call a commune that's made up of each sign of the Zodiac. That is, it will be when it's complete. Right now we have a Gemini, a Cancer, a Libra and a Capricorn. And, of course, an Aries, which is me. It's an all-girl group. We live in a mansion up in the mountains near Mt. Shasta. I was thinking you might want to come up and check us out. Who knows, you might like it."

"Geez, I don't know. I mean, I don't even know you …"

"Sure, you do. I'm the lady who took you off the street and is offering you a place you can call home."

A myriad of thoughts flooded Nancy's mind. Was this the best thing that could ever happen to her or the worst? She might only be fifteen but she was no dummy. She'd heard the stories of white slavers. Was it possible this woman had brought her to this fancy restaurant and bought her the best meal of her life because she was some sort of saint, or could she be looking for fresh meat for a brothel?

"By the way, you aren't a virgin, are you?"

"Should I to be?"

"No, no, certainly not. It's nothing, really. In a way it's better that you aren't. I just wondered."

Thoughts began swirling in Nancy's mind. If she'd had any doubts before about what this so called commune was, Aries last question had pretty much cleared that up.

"Where did you say this place is? Up in the mountains? Like up in Tahoe?" If it was in Tahoe she was definitely not interested. That was where her mother lived, which made it the last place on earth she ever wanted to be.

"No, we're in a completely different mountain range. Like I said, we're near Mt. Shasta, about a hundred miles from the Oregon border. It's not showy like the Tahoe area, but I think you'll like it."

Thinking about what her life would be like if she should turn Aries' offer down - living on the streets, hungry all the time, scared to death to sleep at night - Nancy decided she had nothing to lose by agreeing to go with her new benefactor. Even if it meant giving up her virginity to some loser who couldn't get a girl without paying her, at least she would have a roof over her head and food in her stomach.

"Yeah, that sounds nice. I'll be happy to go with you."

"Wonderful! I know you'll like the other girls. We're all one big family, one big sisterhood. In fact, we like to call ourselves the 'Sisterhood of the Zodiac.' "

"Wow, that's … that's just great. It sounds like it might be fun."

"Well, then, let me welcome you to the family, Scorpio. I just know you're going to love it."

"Scorpio? My name's Nancy."

"Oh, didn't I tell you? We leave our old names behind so we can truly embrace the Zodiac. We only use our signs. That's why we never have more than one person per sign. It makes life so much easier that way."

Nancy was fairly certain of two things when she climbed back into the VW bus. First, the woman who called herself Aries was a complete nutcase. And second, that she, Nancy Hershall-turned-Scorpio, had just agreed to sell her body for a warm place to sleep and food for her stomach.

The four hour drive north gave her plenty of time to reflect on how she had managed to end up virtually giving herself away to a total stranger.

She had never lived the kind of life other kids had. For one thing, she had never even met her father, not even once. For all she knew her mother may not even know who the guy was. Over the years Nancy had come to think of her mother as the queen of the one night stand. Oh, there had been a few guys who stayed around for a few weeks, even a couple who had lasted for a year or more, but for the most part they were in and out so fast the little girl had taken to calling them simply 'Sir,' and leaving it at that.

Her mom had come straight from the farm to Las Vegas with dreams of becoming a glamorous chorus girl. She'd seen pictures of the dancers, all decked out in rhinestones and feathers, strutting their stuff in front of crowds of rich men. She was certain she was every bit as pretty as any of those girls, prettier than a lot of them, if she was being honest about it. Heck, she could even dance a step or two. All she had to do was to get herself to Vegas and she'd be having those guys panting over her in no time.

The only problem with little Anna Marie Hershall's plan was that, although she had been selected to be the Queen of the Corn Husker Festival - and it was the beauty pageant queen, not queen of the actual corn husking - the city of Las Vegas was already loaded with small town beauty queens who also had expectations of wearing those dazzling costumes.

It took her over a year to realize her dream was nothing but just that - a dream. It most likely would have taken her longer to learn that hard lesson had she not discovered she had gone and gotten herself pregnant.

Unfortunately, Anna Marie was a girl with a rather slow brain process, so by the time she realized what had happened, nearly five months past the actual event of conception, there wasn't a lot she could do about the pregnancy except to go through with it.

Which is not to say she didn't try to get rid of it - she did, many times. Her last attempt had resulted in an early birth of a surprisingly healthy baby girl. Left to her own devices, Anna Marie might have still found a way to get rid of the kid but, unfortunately for the mother, and fortunately for Nancy, a concerned neighbor had called 911 after hearing Anna Marie making strange noises through the thin motel walls. Still too weak to figure out a way to dispose of the tiny infant, the mother was soon surrounded by well-meaning and very efficient emergency responders. Before she knew what was happening, she and her baby were loaded into an ambulance and trucked off to the hospital.

What happened next was what caused Nancy to be brought up by a mother who would have done anything to have prevented her birth. Her mother had such poor motherly instincts she would rather have seen her child dead than given to an adoptive family that might actually find it in their heart to love the child she so despised.

The night of the birth was a slow news night in Las Vegas. There had been no traffic accidents of note anywhere near the city. Nor were there any particularly interesting robberies. In fact, other than a couple of disorderly drunken events, 911 had been sitting idle for longer than any of the emergency operators could remember.

It was because of this that Anna Marie finally received her first break. The next morning, while she was still in the hospital, one of the nurses bustled into her room with excitement written all over her expressive face.

"Guess what?" she said, her face lit up with an enormous grin. "You're famous, little momma. There're three news reporters down at the nurse's desk asking for interviews with you. They want to put you on TV!"

It took Anna Marie about two seconds to realize she had just been given the best gift ever. If she played her cards right this nuisance she had given birth to might actually turn out to be her best chance at fame.

"What do you say, honey? Do I call them in or turn them away?"

"Bring 'em on! But, wait," Anna Marie called out before the nurse was through the door, "give me five minutes, okay? Five minutes, then let 'em in. Oh, and can you bring me the baby?"

By the time the reporters were led into her room Anna Marie had combed her hair and applied a particularly flattering shade of lipstick. Leaning back on two pillows, she was cradling her newborn daughter in her arms.

Before they left, the reporters had learned Anna Marie's sad tale. She told them about her aspirations of being a Vegas showgirl and about how her pregnancy had forced her into a financial abyss. She was frantic about how she would ever be able to pay her hospital bills. She didn't know what she would do if she couldn't get the help she needed just long enough for her to find a job that could support not only her but also her precious child.

About half way through her story tears began to well up in her eyes. She let them fall without making any effort at brushing them away. By the time she was finished, her tears were falling on her baby's cheeks. It was not until then that she bothered to dab at them with a tissue … not from her own face, only from the child's. It was a superb performance which was recorded faithfully by two network TV news crews. It was first shown locally early that afternoon, then nationally in the evening. She was receiving gifts and fielding job offers within hours of the first showing.

No one would ever praise Anna Marie's mothering skills the first two years of her daughter's life. But, on the other hand, she was also not the worst mother on earth. For the most part her parenting consisted of finding decent, yet cheap, caregivers to take care of the kid while she went about living the life she had dreamed of. At first money poured in, along with tons of cute baby outfits and toys. She didn't have to worry about a thing while she recovered from the delivery.

Rather than worrying, she spent most of her time trying to decide which job offer to take. The one she eventually chose was so far beyond her expectations she frequently felt like she should pinch herself to see if she wasn't dreaming. Her dream had always been to be one of the chorus girls, but what she was offered was the chance to be the headliner. Suddenly she was being photographed every time she so much as left her apartment - an apartment that was paid for by the show's producer.

She spent one entire day in a salon so expensive she hadn't even known such places existed. The show's producer demanded that she be given the whole treatment: nails, hair, skin care and whatever else they had to offer. When she caught a glimpse of herself in a mirror as she walked out of the salon, her first thought was, 'Who is that gorgeous woman?'

There was only one problem with Anna Marie's explosive new career: the woman had absolutely no talent. Not only that but her beauty, even after her producer had spent a veritable fortune on outfitting her, was still only marginal. After all was said and done, what had been considered remarkable in her rural hometown was seen as just shy of acceptable in Las Vegas. Her career ended up being as fleeting as her fame, which turned out to be just under six months.

The defining moment in her daughter, Nancy's, life was the night when, as soon as she walked off the stage after her last number, Anna Marie was handed a check along with a letter from her boss's attorney which said her contract was being terminated and that she should note that the amount of the check reflected not only the period covering her time on stage but also the amount stated in the contract that she was to receive should the backers of the show decide her services would no longer be needed.

She was shocked, of course, but after seeing the amount of the check her spirits leaped with glee. They didn't want her? Well, she didn't want them! Their show was nothing more than a two-bit piece of shit anyway. They'd been lucky to get her in the first place.

Vowing to deposit the check first thing the next morning before they had a chance to change their minds, she took a cab back to the apartment her producer, more recently her lover, had provided. She slept like a baby until little Nancy woke her early the next morning.

She was humming a tune that nobody with any ear for music would have recognized and pouring herself a cup of coffee when she had her first insight into what was actually happening. There was a knock on her door followed by the voice of the apartment complex's manger.

"Miss Hershall!" she heard his voice call just before he knocked again, this time harder. "If I may speak to you, Miss Hershall?"

What the hell does he want? She wondered as she went to open the door. *Hasn't he received this month's rent yet?*

"If you want your money you're talking to the wrong person," she told him in a rather unpleasant voice. "You ought to know by now I'm not the person you need to talk to about that.

"Actually, you are, *Miss* Hershall."

She hated it when he stressed the *Miss* part of her name, like she was so far below him he'd have to scrape the ground to reach her. "I've come by this morning to give you this, courtesy of the management." He handed her an envelope with the letterhead of the corporation that owned hers and several other Las Vegas apartment complexes. She was holding the envelope when she looked up at him and saw a very satisfied smile on his face.

"Thanks," she said in as sarcastic a tone as she could manage while still saying only the one word. She waited until she was back inside the apartment and had closed the door before she ripped the envelope open.

She couldn't believe her eyes. It was a God-damned eviction notice!

Fighting off panic, she raced to the telephone to call her benefactor. There had to be some mistake. She couldn't possibly have lost her job one day and her apartment the next. Things just didn't happen like that. Didn't they realize they were dealing with Anna Marie Hershall? That she was God damned famous? Crappy stuff like this just didn't happen to famous people. Everybody knew that.

The panic subsided a bit when she recalled the amount of money she had been given the previous night. This was just a bump in the road, as her grandma would have said. She'd find a new job - hell, a better job - so fast those fucking idiots wouldn't know what happened. And she'd get herself another apartment. And it would be better than this one, too. Gazing about the room, she told herself she'd never really liked it all that much, anyway. Next time she'd be the one picking it out and it would make this place look like a God-damned shack.

Finding the new apartment proved to be more difficult than she had expected. It was true she had enough money in the bank to pay for at least a year's lease on a suitable place for her and her daughter, but none of the rental agencies that handled the kind of apartment she was looking for would even consider her application as long as she was unemployed. She finally had to settle for a medium-priced unit in a complex that was clear across town from the Strip, which was hardly in her choice location. Still, she wasn't worried. She wouldn't be there for long. All she had to do was to let the casinos know she was available and her phone would start ringing off the hook.

Unfortunately, her phone never rang. Not one single offer came her way. She had been so sure of herself that, after a week without having the phone ringing even once, she had actually used a neighbor's phone to place a call to herself, certain there must be something wrong with her phone. When she heard her own voice saying how pleased she was that 'they' had called and if they would just leave their name and number she'd get right back to them, she realized it wasn't the phone that was broken; she was what was broken.

The change that came over her then was not gradual. It came at her like one of the torrential storms that had so often come across the prairie towards her home town, threatening to destroy all in its path. Only this time it wasn't just a threat. This time the storm meant business. This time, instead of bending with the wind, she stood stiff as it buffeted her one way and then another, until she lay trembling in a heap of despair. This time she was destroyed.

With her own destruction came her daughter's, which was only right, as far as Anna Marie was concerned. After all, if she didn't have to worry about taking care of that whiney little brat she would be able to go anywhere, do anything. By the time she was through placating herself for all she had lost she had come to realize that everything bad that had happened could be laid at Nancy's feet. She should have aborted the little piece of puke right at the beginning.

From that day forward Nancy's life turned into just one day after another of abuse, both physical and mental. Plain neglect would have been a blessing; to be neglected would have meant that she was simply being ignored - she might have learned to tolerate neglect. But the abuse was something she would never get used to.

Her mother was always smart enough to never leave marks on her daughter that could not be explained away. A quick but painful pinch here or there were her preferred means of controlling Nancy, along with a frequent trip or shove. Anna Marie would laugh uproariously when she managed to throw Nancy off balance enough so that the little girl would go flying and end up sprawled on the floor. "Get up, you clumsy oaf," she would taunt.

Actually, Nancy *was* a clumsy child and so shy the thought of attending a new school whenever her mother was kicked out of her apartment, which happened so often her daughter lost count of how many schools she attended, just about paralyzed her.

Not only did they move from one apartment to another, they also moved from one city to another.

They left Las Vegas in the dark of night so suddenly Nancy was barely aware they were actually leaving town until the city lights faded away behind them. When she saw nothing but desert ahead of them she finally realized she would not be going to school that morning. She sat in the backseat of her mom's most recent boyfriend's car surrounded by blankets, clothing and her only doll.

From what she heard of the two adults' conversation she began to suspect he had done something bad and needed to get out of town without anyone knowing. When he promised to give her mother money for coming along and making it look like he was part of a family, instead of just a guy on his own, she figured he must be in a lot of trouble. She spent most of the trip to Reno worrying that if he was in trouble did it mean she and her mother were in trouble, too?

Leaving Reno was far less dramatic. This time her mother was promised a job at a new casino in Tahoe. Anna Marie wasn't exactly sure what the job was but she hoped she would be doing it on a stage with a bunch of other ladies. Unfortunately, the job offer had come from a guy who was more interested in getting Anna Marie in bed than giving her a job. Apparently he hadn't heard how easy that would have been even without the job offer. A few drinks and even more compliments and she would have done just about anything for or to him.

Of course, from Anna Marie's perspective, everything bad that happened was all her daughter's fault. If she didn't have to take care of the brat she could go anywhere and be anything. After a couple of Coke and rums, the pinching and slapping would start. Nancy had become so accustomed to it she took the abuse as her due. Maybe if she wasn't so clumsy and ugly her mommy would be happier. And if she was happier maybe she wouldn't drink that stuff so much. She might even find a man who would stay around long enough to be a daddy.

She knew that along with being clumsy she was probably the ugliest girl in her new classroom, probably in the whole new school. She couldn't remember her mother ever telling her she was pretty, or even just plain. It had always been, "How could someone as beautiful as me have ended up with a thing like you?" Or, "I hope you realize you didn't inherit your looks from me. It was your dad that made you so ugly. If he hadn't been rich I never would have let him near me." The insults were constant and insidious. After a while Nancy accepted them as truth, never looking into a mirror if she could avoid it.

Fortunately, the one type of abuse she had never had to endure was sexual. Although her mother frequently allowed men to live with them, as a sexually demanding woman she had always managed to satisfy her partners' sexual urges.

During her adolescent years, however, Nancy began hearing stories from her classmates about men who were drawn to girls of her age, men who hungered after being the guy who took a young girl's virginity. Her awareness of what her mother was doing with all the men who trafficked through their home suddenly became ominous. That was when she started locking her bedroom door and hiding a long butcher knife under her pillow every night.

The nights when her mother and her date would return home, both obviously drunk, were the most frightening for her. She was familiar with her mother's drinking patterns; how quickly her mother could go from being the life of the party to passing out and sleeping it off wherever she happened to be. Those were the nights Nancy dreaded the most.

Even though her mother had convinced her daughter she was so ugly no man would ever look at her, Nancy still worried that if a guy was drunk enough he might not care what she looked like. After years of observing her mother and her friends' drinking habits, she had come to the realization that there were never any absolutes when it came to drunks. They just couldn't be trusted, no matter what a girl looked like.

Then one day she took a real look at herself in the bathroom mirror. What she saw was a very unkempt girl, but not an ugly one. It was true she hadn't taken after her mother with her silvery blond hair and sky blue eyes. Apparently she had taken after her father, a man who might have been Italian or perhaps of Spanish decent. Her hair was long and straight, and was such a dark brown it could be mistaken as coal black. Her eyes were blue, but not like her mother's. There was an intensity to the color of her eyes that her mother's lacked. Their slight lift at their outer corners gave the impression that she might also have a drop or two of oriental blood in her.

Someone who understood about such things might have told her that her facial features were in perfect proportion: Her nose was straight and just the right length; her mouth was lush, yet not overly so; her complexion was sallow, but that was to be expected considering her living conditions. A good diet and plenty of sunshine would take care of that in no time.

It was at that moment that she realized why her mother hated her so much: She wasn't ugly, she was beautiful, far more beautiful than her mother ever had been. If she wanted to she could be the one who attracted the men, not her mother. She was her mother's competition.

That was the day she realized that one day very soon she would have to find a way to escape her mother's influence. It was when she began to hoard every cent she could get her hands on. Up until then she had handed over all of her baby sitting money to her mother. Now she began to find ways of keeping at least some of it.

It wasn't all that difficult. More often than not her mother was either working a night shift as a cocktail waitress or drinking herself blind with whatever guy she'd picked up earlier in the night. For the most part she did not know, nor did she care, what her daughter did while she was away from home. All she cared about was seeing the money on her nightstand that Nancy left for her when she returned from babysitting. Knowing that, Nancy continued leaving money; she just didn't leave all of it.

When Nancy came to the realization of why her mother treated her so badly she was filled with rage, an emotion she had never known before. Since the emotion was new to her, she didn't know what to do with it. She had suffered humiliation and pain for so many years they had become her normal. Now all that had changed.

Always a loner, now she spent even more time in her tiny room. Every moment when she was not in school or out babysitting she sat in front of her mirror studying her face, her hair, her blossoming body. Nearly sixteen years old, she had somehow turned into a woman without even realizing it.

For the first time in her life Nancy began to take pleasure in baiting her mother. Using a portion of her own money, she started shopping for herself. She went to the nearest variety store to buy cosmetics. The girls she knew at school who were wearing makeup tended to use light shades of lipstick and even a bit of mascara. That was not what Nancy had in mind. When she walked out of that store she was carrying the blackest mascara she could find, along with a matching eyeliner. She had also bought a lipstick so red it could have been seen from a mile away.

Nancy felt rage bubbling up from deep within her as she applied the makeup with a heavy hand the next morning. She could hardly wait to see the look on her mother's face when she saw her 'ugly' daughter now. She slammed around the apartment, making as much noise as she could, hoping to wake her mother, but without success. She knew she shouldn't have expected her mother to be awake at such an early hour but she was frustrated as she clambered down the steps after slamming the front door with all the energy she could summon.

The looks she got at school bothered her at first, but it didn't take long for her anger at her mother to reach out to include everyone who so much as glanced at her. What the fuck was wrong with them? By the time she arrived back home her rage had built to a fever pitch. If her mother wasn't home she'd damn well check every bar in town until she found her.

Nancy entered the apartment, slamming the door as hard as she could.

"Hey! Keep it down, will ya?" Her mother came shuffling out of the kitchen, dressed in her ratty robe, holding a mug of coffee in her hand. It was a moment or two before she actually looked at her daughter. "What the hell?"

"What's the matter, mother? Don't like what you see?" Nancy taunted.

"I never have and I never will. Now, go wash that junk off your face. You look like a damned whore."

"No."

"What the hell to you mean, 'no'?

"I mean *no*. I like how I look, so you better get used to it, old lady"

Coffee flew across the room as Anna Marie lunged toward her daughter, her hand raised, ready to slap Nancy's face, but before she knew what was happening Nancy had grabbed her mother's wrist and pulled her toward her until their faces were just inches apart.

"Don't ever hit me again."

"I'll damn well do whatever I want. You can't just come in here and take over. I'm still -"

"Still what, mother? Still going to slam me around whenever you feel like it?" She had heard the expression 'blind with rage' before, now she knew what it meant. Without thinking what she was doing, she released her mother's arm, pulled her hand back and slapped her mother's face as hard as she could.

Something happened to her as she gazed into her mother's shocked face. Standing this close, filled with the rage that had been building for longer than she knew, she suddenly realized how much taller she was than her mother. She was taller and more powerful.

"You might want to clean that coffee off the carpet. If you don't, it's going to leave an awful stain." There was no mistaking the taunt in her voice.

"But …"

"Don't even think I'm doing it for you. From now on, old lady, you're on your own. I'm just here for the ride."

The confrontation was brief, yet effective. Nancy had taken away her mother's power and never gave it back.

Things remained fairly quiet at the Hershall home for quite a while after that. It wasn't a peaceful quiet, nor was there any love shown between the two women, but as long as Anna Marie left Nancy alone, they managed to get through each day without conflict. Nancy continued to dress and groom herself to her own satisfaction, which in truth did appear to be rather trashy. And, Anna Marie came and went without so much as glancing her daughter's way.

It might have continued that way forever had Karl Sutherfield not entered the picture.

Karl was a loud-mouthed, hard-drinking guy her mother picked up one night at the bar where she worked. She brought him home that night and he simply never left. He had been a handsome man at one time but his body had gone to fat and his hair was long, gray and greasy. From what Nancy could see, his only attributes must be kept in the bedroom. Otherwise, she couldn't figure out what her mother saw in him.

At first he tried chatting Nancy up, trying to win her over with charm. After a few days of her hateful looks and bad attitude he finally backed off. But still, when he thought she wasn't looking, she caught him staring at her. She didn't like the way he looked at her, like she was a big dish of ice cream and he wanted to gobble her up. It was then that she returned to locking her bedroom door and slipping the butcher knife under her pillow at night.

It happened one night just weeks after Nancy's sixteenth birthday, which had passed without any celebration, much like all of the other birthdays she could remember. Her mother dressed for work as usual. Before she left she checked with Karl about when he would be coming to the bar. They often went there together but this night he said there was something he wanted to watch on the TV and he would be coming later.

Nancy spent the evening in her room listening to music and finishing up a report that was due for her history class the next morning. History was one of her favorite subjects, so she was so involved in the report she forgot all about locking her door. She was just closing her book when she thought she heard someone outside her bedroom door. It was only a slight sound, but still something just didn't feel right. She was just rising from the bed when the door burst open, revealing the naked body of her mother's latest lover.

The scuffle that ensued was a silent one. He was completely absorbed in his attempt to remove her clothes; she was just as absorbed in fighting him off and figuring out how she was going to get to her knife. She was a strong five foot seven - but still she was no match for his superior bulk. He flung her to the bed and was pinning her upper body to the mattress while trying to pull down her panties when they both heard Anna Marie's screeching voice.

"I knew it!" Then there was the whapping sound of a broom handle hitting the bed next to Nancy's head. "Get off her, you son of a bitch!" The broom handle caught him right across the buttocks. "Get in our bedroom and put some clothes on!" Another whap, this time across Nancy's bare thigh. "And you, you little whore, can get your ass out of my house! Go on!" she yelled even louder as she continued beating her daughter with the boom handle until Nancy finally managed to wrench the weapon away from her mother and throw it against the wall where Anna Marie couldn't get to it without going past her daughter.

"Get out," her mother hissed into her daughter's face. "Get out and don't ever come back."

Nancy straightened her clothes, grabbed her purse and a jacket, and was outside the door in mere moments. She was down the stairs and onto the sidewalk before it hit her that she had no idea where she was going or what she was going to do.

It was early summer, so although she was in the high mountains of Tahoe, Nevada, it wouldn't be too cold as long as she had her jacket. And, thankfully, she always kept her entire savings in her purse, knowing that if she tried to hide it in the apartment her mother was sure to find it while Nancy was away. She had nearly thirty-five dollars, surely enough to get her by until she found a job.

Her first thought was to get away from Tahoe as soon as possible. Her mother had let her know she would not be welcome there ever again. Ha! As if she would ever *want* to go home. As far as she was concerned, the farther she could get from her mother, the better.

The south shore of Tahoe on the Nevada side of the state line was pretty much a twenty-four hour area. The casinos, while not being as grand as those in Las Vegas, or even like the ones in Reno, were still happening places. They were kept lit as bright as day around the clock, although you would not find a clock in any of them because time was meaningless when you were having fun, right?

It didn't take Nancy long to leave her quiet neighborhood and arrive at the glittering tourist area. One thing her mom had made sure of whenever they moved to a new town was that they lived near the casinos, just in case she might have to walk to work. Her lifestyle being what it was, owning a running vehicle was more than a chancy thing. Walking was fine, except in winter when it snowed. That was when Anna Marie was even more likely to have a handy man sharing her bed, one who owned a car.

The closer Nancy got to the bright lights of the casinos, the better she felt. She'd show that fucking bitch! She wouldn't waste her life getting drunk every night then sleeping with whatever creep brought her home. She'd get a real job, someplace where people dressed nice and treated each other like human beings. She didn't know how she was going to do it, but that was all right, she knew she had what it took to make it. She just had to find out what it was she was looking for. In the meantime, she had to get out of the mountains and into a city.

Considering where she was starting from, her city of choice, at least at that moment, was Sacramento. It was the closest city big enough to give her the opportunities she was looking for and, even better, it was not in Nevada. Her mother had pretty much ruined the state for her. If she had anything to do with it, she would never step foot in it again.

It took her almost three hours to find a ride down the mountain. She could have gone sooner, but the only people who offered to take her were men who had the same look in their eyes Karl had. She'd stayed a virgin this long. She was not about to give it up for something as cheap as a car ride.

She finally spotted a group who met her criteria. They were clearly all college-aged kids off for a night of fun in the glittering Tahoe casinos. She spotted the three girls and one guy leaving one of the casinos, laughing together at one of their winnings and all of the others' losses. The conversation she overheard indicated their intention of returning home that night. Walking over to them, she asked for a ride if they were headed toward Sacramento. Without batting an eye they invited her to join them. Squeezed into the back seat between two of the girls, she headed down the mountain on Interstate Fifty, leaving her past behind. Life could only get better from here on out.

Of course, things had not gone as easily for her as she had hoped. It seemed she was too young for a job at fast food stores. The same was true when she applied for waitressing jobs, as well as any other sort of store clerk work. When she discovered how expensive even the worst looking motel was, she followed the advice of one of the motel clerks and made her way to the Greyhound station. The bench she chose to sleep on was far from comfortable, but for the most part she felt safe there.

It took her three days to run out of money, three days of trying to find work while eating as little as possible. By that time she realized her time at the bus station had come to an end. If she tried to stay there one more night she was sure someone would report her to the police as a possible runaway. It was a wonder it hadn't happened yet. It was then that she met Aries, her salvation - at least she hoped she had been saved. She would soon discover if the place Aries was taking her was any better than the one she had so recently escaped.

Chapter 21

After they finished their meal Aries took Nancy back to the VW bus. Within half-an-hour they had left Sacramento and were heading north on the I-5. Sated by the enormous meal she had consumed, the young girl slipped easily into a deep, dreamless sleep. She might have slept all the way to Dunsmuir, a three-and-a-half hour drive, if Aries hadn't stopped at a Walmart along the way to purchase an entire new wardrobe for Nancy.

As she noted the clothing Aries was tossing into the shopping cart, the younger girl wondered once again what sort of place she was heading to. If it was a brothel, it must be a lot different than how she had envisioned such a place would be. Rather than the skimpy, shear clothing she imagined the working girls would wear in a whorehouse, the items that were beginning to fill the cart were far more utilitarian. There were three pairs of jeans, one size larger than the tight ones she was wearing, and half a dozen T-shirts. Plain cotton panties and bras, two nightgowns, a package of white cotton socks and a pair of sneakers completed their purchases.

Nancy had never owned as many clothes at any one time as they had just purchased. And they were all new! Not one thing had come from the thrift store, which was where her mother usually bought her daughter's clothing.

When she had agreed to go with Aries, Nancy had done so believing she was most likely selling herself to the first bidder, that no matter how nice the woman was there had to be bad news at the end of the rainbow. Now she didn't know what to think. She had never eaten such a fantastic meal as the one Aries had bought her, the back seat was loaded with brand new clothing for her, and now they were headed up to what this lady called a 'mansion.' Could she really be this lucky?

It was early evening when they finally drove into Dunsmuir. They turned off the highway onto Dunsmuir Avenue, and made a right hand turn at the town's city hall. One short block brought them to Sacramento Avenue, where they had to turn either north or south. Making a right hand turn, the bus passed a few commercial buildings before Aries pulled into a small parking lot.

"Well, here we are," she said as she set the break and stepped out. "Give me a hand with your things," she called as she opened the back passenger door and began pulling out sack after sack of Nancy's new clothes.

Aries' voice brought Nancy out of her shocked state. Man, oh, man, the building was different than she had imagined. But it was beautiful, all the same. When Aries used the word 'mansion' to describe the house, the only points of reference to the word for Nancy were palatial houses she had seen on TV.

This place was huge, but it was not exactly what she would call palatial. If she was being honest, she'd have to describe the building as being a little scary. It was the sort of place where you'd expect to find ghosts.

She was smiling to herself at her whimsical imagination as she climbed the broad wooden steps, her arms so full of clothing she could barely see over them.

"I did mention that this place used to be a mortuary, didn't I?" Aries asked from a couple of steps behind her.

Nancy's eyes widened - but she kept her silence. It was a mansion, she told herself, and that was all that mattered. A mortuary? Aries must be teasing.

When she entered the foyer, her eyes widened even more. She had never seen such a beautiful room in her entire life, not even on TV. There was so much for her to take in: The shiny hardwood floors with their gorgeous oriental rugs; the enormous pillows scattered everywhere; and the rainbow-colored curtains that covered the huge windows.

Her breath caught in her throat when she heard the gentle chiming of a lavishly carved grandfather clock. None of this could be real!

"Come along, Scorpio," Aries called to her, leading her to a wide stairwell. "You must be exhausted. I'll take you to your room and show you where your bathroom is. Why don't you take a good long soak while I have one of the girls bring a dinner tray to your room? I know you're curious to see the whole place but tomorrow will be soon enough for the grand tour."

Nancy followed silently, too amazed to respond.

"Here you are," Aries said as she opened one of the doors on the second floor. "I'm afraid it's the smallest room we have, and it doesn't have its own bath like most of the others do, but the good side to that is when we get our full complement of Zodiac girls, you won't have to share. Well, you will have to share the bathroom, but at least your bedroom will be all yours."

Aries tossed the bags of clothes on the bed. Returning to the hall, she said, "Over here is your bathroom." She opened the door just a step away from Nancy's new room. "You'll find everything you need," she continued, "towels, shampoo, conditioner, even bottles of bubble bath."

It was beyond anything Nancy had ever imagined. The room might have come directly out of a period film with its Victorian claw foot tub. She didn't hear one more word of Aries' descriptive dialogue. All she knew was she wanted to fill that gorgeous tub with hot water and sweet-smelling bubble bath, and soak for at least an hour. If this was what a bordello was, she was happy to be part of it.

As soon as Aries left her alone, Nancy went to her room, rooted out one of the new nightgowns and returned to the bathroom. In no time at all she was leaning back in a tub of hot, foamy suds, glorying in the most delicious bath she had ever experienced. When she realized she was about to fall asleep, she dipped her head into the water, then gave her hair a good scrubbing.

She entered her room a few moments later to discover that, in her absence, someone had placed a tray of sandwiches and milk on the nightstand next to her bed. She couldn't help but wonder why she was being treated like a celebrity. She was just a kid who slept in a bus station. How could she possibly deserve all this?

She awoke the next morning to a light tapping on the door. She opened it to a skinny girl of about her own age. "Hi, Scorpio, I'm Aquarius. Aries asked me to bring you down for breakfast. Then after we clean up the kitchen, I can give you a tour of the whole house."

Nancy grabbed the first pair of jeans and t-shirt she touched and slipped into them. After running a comb through her hair and brushing her teeth, she followed the girl back down the stairs.

"Did you sleep alright?" Aquarius asked. "Sometimes people hear odd things at night here. I hope you weren't scared."

"If there were any odd noises last night they were probably me," Nancy laughed. "I don't think I've ever slept so hard."

"Don't tell me you talk in your sleep!"

"Only when I get really tired. I just hope I don't say things I wouldn't want anyone else to hear. You know, that could really be embarrassing."

They had reached the dining room where a full breakfast was laid out boarding house style. Several other girls sat at the table eating their breakfasts while they discussed their upcoming workday. Was this how regular people lived? If so, Nancy was thrilled to be part of it.

Chapter 22

Aries left the next morning on what she called a hunting expedition' without leaving any specific instructions for Nancy who helped her load up two more paintings and a pair of sterling silver candlesticks into the bus. After she'd watched the wildly painted bus turn up towards Dunsmuir Avenue and out of view, Nancy returned to the house.

She went to the kitchen where she found Libra and Aquarius washing the breakfast dishes. Picking up a dishtowel, she began helping to dry the breakfast plates.

"It sure would be nice if this place had a dishwasher, wouldn't it?" she asked as a way of breaking the silence that had settled over the room when she entered it.

"Yeah, but back when this old place was built no one had ever heard of dishwashers."

"We don't mind doing it, do we, Libra? It gives us time to visit for a while before we each go on to our other work."

"And what would that be?"

"Oh, different stuff. Libra and I take care of the house. You know, clean, cook, all that kind of stuff. The other girls have jobs outside. Libra and I like staying home with Aries.

"After we're finished in here I'll show you around the place. I know it must feel like a big old mausoleum, which since it used to be a mortuary, it kind of is. But it won't take you long before you'll be able to find your way around."

"After you two get done with the grand tour, don't forget we need to get you moved into my room today," Aquarius said to Libra. "Maybe you can help us do that, Scorpio."

"Sure, but why do you guys have to give up your privacy? I thought Aries said there were enough bedrooms for everyone to have their own."

"Oh, I guess you didn't understand what Aries meant when she said she was going hunting! She's off looking for some more girls for the Sisterhood. She usually brings two girls at a time. You're the first one to come alone. We don't have any more empty bedrooms, so Libra and I offered to bunk together."

"Aquarius and I have been friends from when we were just little kids. I'm actually looking forward to bunking with her. I never did like being so far away from her, way down the hall and on the other side of the house, and all."

"Yeah, Libra wants me around to scare away all the ghosts," Aquarius teased.

"Hey, watch it!" Libra replied as she snapped a dishtowel at her friend.

Nancy watched the play between the two girls. They were behaving just like in her favorite TV shows. This house seemed more like a home than any place she had ever lived.

She had a hundred questions about what the so-called 'Sisterhood' was all about but decided that it was too soon to be to be asking a lot of questions. From what she'd seen so far, even though it still felt a little odd, there didn't seem to be anything wrong with how everyone was living here. Maybe she'd actually landed in a little bit of heaven, after all.

By the time Libra finished showing her throughout the house Nancy was certain she would never be able to find herself around without a guide, but Libra assured her she'd know the place from top to bottom in no time at all.

"I noticed that we didn't check out the basement or the attic. Are they off limits?"

"Oh, you'll be seeing the attic soon enough, but we don't need to go there today. The basement, that's another matter. Now that you've mentioned it, I don't think anyone's actually been down there. It's locked up pretty tight, so I guess Aries figured it wasn't worth bothering with."

Nancy wondered how the basement had not grabbed everyone's curiosity. A basement in a mortuary? There had to be something down there worth checking out. But, considering how big the house was, maybe they just hadn't gotten around to bothering with it yet.

Later that day Aries returned with two girls who she introduced as Leo and Capricorn. Both girls were taken directly to Libra's former bedroom, where they stayed until they came down for breakfast the next morning.

Nancy went to bed that night wondering just where she fit in this so-called Sisterhood. Libra and Aquarius appeared to have the house taken care of. The new girls were both old enough to find outside work. She couldn't imagine what she had to offer. Leo and Capricorn were both a bit older than the others and, from what she overheard, had some kind of work experience which would make it easy for them to find jobs. She worried that if she couldn't find a way to make herself useful, Aries might regret bringing her to Dunsmuir. She panicked at the thought that she might be sent packing when it was discovered that, other than doing a little babysitting, she hadn't worked a day in her life.

Chapter 23

"After we're finished here, I'd like you to take Scorpio up to Eddy," Aries told Aquarius the next evening at the dinner table. "You can take her with you when you take him his dinner."

Nancy's eyes widened with curiosity. *Eddy? There was a guy here?* And, if he didn't eat here with everyone else, what was wrong with him? Her head was filled with questions but she managed to keep silent. She'd spent a lifetime learning to bring as little attention to herself as possible. It was a habit she would not soon forget.

Back in the kitchen she watched as Libra packed a hearty dinner onto a tray, which she then covered it with a tea towel.

"All ready," she said as she handed it to Aquarius.

"Thanks," Aquarius responded as she took the heavily laden tray. "Come along, my little pretty," she said to Nancy in a very 'Wicked Witch of the West' voice. Then, grinning at Nancy's wide-eyed reaction, she turned and left the room. Heading up what the girls called the servant's staircase, she glanced over her shoulder to see that her charge was following.

"Don't worry about Eddy," she said when she saw the worried expression on Nancy's face. "He's a pretty nice guy. Actually, we all like him a lot."

"If he's so nice, why do you guys keep him up in the attic? Is he retarded or something?"

"God, you have such a great imagination!" Libra laughed. "No, he's not 'retarded or something.' There's nothing wrong with him except that he probably smokes too much pot. Other than that, he's the guy that takes care of the Sisterhood's needs, if you get my meaning."

Nancy did not get Libra's meaning but was not about to admit to being so dense.

"Does he stay up there all the time? I mean, do you guys let him out or anything?

"Of course he gets out. He has a job, and, oh, I don't know, I guess he goes out whenever he wants to. But he's always there when we need him. And, guess what - tonight's your turn to need him!"

Nancy stopped still. *Need him?* Why would she need him, or any other guy, for that matter? Suddenly it dawned on her. For a split second she was certain her stomach was about to lose a very good dinner.

"Hey, what's wrong?" she heard Libra ask from the landing at the top of the stairs.

"Huh? Uh, nu ... Um, I was just thinking that maybe I should have brought something with me. You know, like ... like maybe a nightgown?"

"Oh, my God, you are so funny!" Libra laughed. "Don't worry about it, darlin'. You will most definitely not need a nightgown tonight." This comment was followed by an exaggerated wink.

"Take it from me you're going to love our Eddy. Now, come on, let's get the two of you acquainted."

With the words *you're going to love our Eddy* echoing in her mind, Nancy went up the last few steps feeling like a lamb being led to the slaughter.

"Open up in there", Libra called out soon as she reached the top of the stairs. Nancy had no doubt she was about to meet the man who would take her virginity. She fought the urge to throw up as she listened to footsteps coming toward them from the other side of the door.

She almost lost the battle when the door was suddenly flung open. "Welcome, gorgeous! I thought you'd never … Oh, you've got someone with you."

Libra stepped aside, allowing Eddy to get his first good look at Nancy. She was amused to note that for the first time since she had known him, Eddy Sudcliff appeared to be struck dumb.

"Eddy, Scorpio. Scorpio, Eddy. There, I've made the introductions. The rest of the night is up to you two."

Before Nancy could register what was happening, Libra had set the tray on a nearby table and left the apartment, closing the door very firmly behind her.

At first they simply stood there gazing at one another. Feeling the silence closing in on her, Nancy finally broke it by saying, "You probably ought to eat." Then, to her complete embarrassment, she felt the heat of an intense blush radiating from her face as she suddenly recalled some of the raunchier descriptions she'd heard about what went on during sexual intercourse. Why did she have to say that word? *Eat* … talk about a *double entendre*! "I mean, you know, before it gets cold."

His slow, easy grin only made her face feel hotter. She began to wonder how long they would stand there staring at one another. How did these thing go? Was she supposed to do something, say something, to let him know she was ready to … to what?

"Yeah, I guess I really ought to eat," he finally said as his grin spread even wider. Then, without another comment, he turned to the small dining room table and pulled out a chair.

"Why don't you sit with me," he said, indicating that she should sit in the chair he held. "Maybe you'd like to share some of this with me. The Sisters always give me enough food to feed an army. It'd be a shame to waste any of it."

"I, uh, I already ate."

Not knowing what else to do, she sat in the chair he held for her and allowed him to push it under the table.

"So, how do you like the setup here?"

"It's okay, I guess."

Once again the room was filled with silence. Eddy looked across the table at her, apparently waiting for her to say more.

As the silence stretched out he turned his attention to his meal, which he devoured with amazing speed.

When he had finished eating Nancy rose from the table, took the dirty dishes over to the sink and began washing them. Eddy stayed where he was, watching her every move.

"And, uh, what do you think about Dunsmuir?"

"Not much. Oh, I don't mean how that sounded. It's not like I don't like the town. What I meant was I haven't left the house since I got here, so I don't know if I like it or not."

"That's great! I mean, it's great that I can show you around. Come on, let's get out of here. It's my day off and I haven't been out of my apartment since we … uh, I mean … since I got out of bed. I could use a little fresh air."

He would have to mention the word 'bed', she thought as she hung the wet dishtowel on its rack. She'd managed to forget for a whole couple of minutes why she'd been brought here. Now it was right out there in the open. *Damn!*

If she'd met him under other circumstances she figured she might have actually been drawn to the guy, even though he was really, really, old. He could be twenty-five, maybe even older! But he was kind'a cute.

"Are you coming?" he called from the opened outside door.

Following him down the steep steps, she felt her nerves begin to relax. If she had to give up her virginity, doing it with this guy might not be too bad.

As they walked through the commercial district of Dunsmuir, looking into windows, sometimes going into the stores to look closer at their merchandise, Eddy found himself entranced with the young girl Libra had brought him. She was unbelievably beautiful, yet she seemed to be unaware of it. In some ways she appeared shy, in others worldly beyond her years. It was difficult for him to believe that what they would be doing together after they returned to his place would be legal in the state of California. Was she truly over seventeen?

She must be or Aries wouldn't have sent her to him. The agreement the two of them had made - that Aries would keep him in weed, groceries and all the sex he wanted - was clear enough. Nowhere in it had there been even the slightest hint that, other than smoking a little pot - oh, alright, a lot of pot - would she ever expect him to break any laws, such as having sex with an under-aged kid. He had a lot of faults but being a pervert wasn't one of them.

The thing was, he was really attracted to the girl. Her innocence touched him. Of course, they'd just met, but he felt like she was someone he would like to get to know as a friend, not just as another sex partner.

"What's your real name, Scorpio?"

"Nancy," she said so softly he could barely hear her.

"Just 'Nancy'? No last name?"

A cloud came over her eyes as she slowly shook her head from side to side and said, "Not anymore. I had one, but I'll never, ever use it again."

Her response, so sparsely yet firmly stated, told him volumes. He wrapped one arm around her shoulders, not pulling her close, letting her know he cared about her in a brotherly sort of way, rather than a lover's. They walked back to the house like that until they came to the narrow outside stairs that led up to his apartment.

He'd made his mind up while they had been walking through town. This Nancy with no last name was not like the others. She was not someone he would take to bed one night then forget in the morning. She was special.

"You know, we don't have to … well, you know …" he said after they entered the apartment.

"Did I do something wrong? I thought you liked me."

"Ah, Scorpio, I like you more than I can say. That's not what I meant at all."

"Then why …?"

"Look, kid, I'm going to ask you something and I want you to promise to tell me the truth, okay?"

Looking solemnly into his eyes, she nodded her head in assent.

"You're still a virgin, aren't you?"

"Am not!" Her heart beat so hard she could actually feel it pounding in her chest. How did he know?

"The truth?"

"No! I mean it. I've done it lots of times! So many times I forgot all the guys I've done it with."

He just smiled at her, shaking his head, telling her without words that he didn't believe a word she was saying.

In spite of her determination not to cry, she could not stop the tears from welling up in her eyes.

"Okay, my little nymphomaniac, let's sit down and talk about this."

Taking her hand, he led her into the living room and sat her down on a Victorian settee. He sat at the other end, turning toward her so he could watch the expressions in her eyes.

"You must know that if we go into that bedroom and make love, I'll know for a fact whether what you're saying is the truth or a lie, don't you?"

One tear slipped over her lower eyelid and cascaded down her cheek. She nodded her answer.

"I'm going to find out that you've been lying, aren't I?"

Once again she nodded. Now a steady stream of tears were flowing down her cheeks.

"Then tell me, why on earth didn't you tell me the truth?"

"Aries doesn't want any virgins here, that's why," she whispered. "If she finds out I lied about it she'll make me leave."

"And you don't have any place to go, is that it?"

Another nod, this time more emphatic than before.

"Well, then, let's not tell her."

"You'd do that?"

"Sure! For the life of me I can't figure out why Aries should have any say in whether a girl is a virgin or not. Personally, I think her caring one way or the other about it is kind of weird."

That statement brought the shadow of a smile to Nancy's lovely face.

"I'll tell you what we're going to do. From now on, you and I are going to be friends ... just friends. Whenever she sends you up here we'll talk, watch a little TV, maybe play a hand or two of cards. You'll stay the night because she'll expect you to. I'll sleep on this couch and you can have my bed. We can enjoy each other's company without Aries having a say in how we do it. Do we have a deal?"

Nancy's face was wreathed in smiles, her moist eyes gleaming with happiness. "We have a deal, except for one thing. You sleep in your bed, I'll sleep here. This thing is so short your legs would hang over the end."

They both slept that night with warm hearts. He hadn't realized how lonely he had been before he'd met Nancy. Plenty of sex was one thing, but a friendship was something else entirely.

For Nancy it was the first night she had ever spent knowing she had an honest-to-God friend.

Chapter 24

ARIES

It was a few minutes past midnight. Libra and Aquarius were once again sitting in front of their Zodiac signs outside the circle on Aries' bedroom floor. Eleven red candles shimmered on the altar behind small glass skulls. A twelfth skull and candle had been placed on the floor in front of Aries, inside the Zodiac circle. The flickering candle flames forming dancing shadows throughout the room lent the scene a sense of eeriness.

"Have you brought your offerings?" Aries asked, glancing from first one girl and then the other.

"We have," both girls whispered as they reached their hands toward their leader, each one bearing a small item.

"Place them in the center of the circle."

When her order had been followed, Aries leaned forward so she could see what gifts had been brought. Seeing both a diamond ring and a man's diamond encrusted Citizen wrist watch, she nodded her acceptance.

"These will do," she said as she scooped both items up off the floor. She rose and took the jewelry to the altar behind her. Bowing her head, she whispered words neither of the girls could hear before placing each gift before a candle.

Turning back to the girls she said, "The Sisterhood accepts your offerings. You will be blessed not only for the value of your gifts but even more so for your valor in obtaining them. Tell me the story of how you obtained your offering, Libra."

Libra's eyes shifted briefly to Aquarius, then back to Aries. "We did it together, Aries. I hope that was okay."

Aries merely bowed her head briefly, as if by doing so she was giving her blessing. When she returned her gaze to Libra, the girl continued with her story.

"We took them from the Mayor's house. We did it on Wednesday night, the night when we knew he and his wife always go to their church's prayer services. We hid behind some bushes at the side of their house until they got into their car and drove away. Then we climbed the fence into the backyard."

"It was so much easier than we'd thought it would be," Aquarius took up the story. "They'd left one of the dining room windows open, so all we had to do was to pop the screen, climb up on one of their outdoor chairs and slip through."

"They don't have any kids or anything, so we weren't worried about anyone else being home."

"Of course, we'd been watching them for a couple of weeks so we knew their schedule and that they lived alone. We didn't want to take any chances on getting caught and bringing any trouble back here," Aquarius emphasized.

"We brought little flashlights, so it wasn't hard to find their bedroom and go through their stuff," Libra added. "Mr. Albritton must not have thought too much of his watch, 'cuz he'd left it right out in plain view. I snatched it up quick. While I was doing that, Aquarius was going through Mrs. Abritton's jewelry box. That's where she found the ring."

"I thought about taking more stuff, but figured if we took just the two things it might be awhile before either one of them noticed they were gone. The ring looked like the best thing in the jewelry case, anyway."

Aries waited a moment or two to see if either of the girls had anything they wanted to add. When they both just sat there gazing at the floor, she assumed they were finished retelling the story of their adventure.

"Tell me, Aquarius, how did you feel when you were going through the Mayor's house?" Aries asked.

"It was like nothing I've ever felt before. I was so excited! I'd do it again in a minute!"

"And you, Libra? What were you feeling when you were stealing Mr. Albritton's watch?"

"I was just hoping it was a good enough gift to get me into the Sisterhood. I didn't care about anything else."

Aries leaned back, a pleased smile gracing her face. "You both did very well. I am pleased with your offerings, and even more so with how you handled yourselves. It makes me proud to take you to the next step."

She rose and turned to the altar where she removed two of the glass skulls. Walking around the outside of the circle, she stopped when she reached each girl so she could bend down and place a skull directly in front of the appropriate Zodiac sign. After placing both skulls she continued around the circle until she had come, once again, to her own sign.

Sitting down before her own skull she addressed the girls once again. "This next step will not only bring you full membership in the Sisterhood, it will identify which of you will receive the honor of being the second-in-charge, following me. The other, by default, will be third."

She noted the pleased glances the two girls exchanged between themselves. Although neither one of them had ever shown any particular outstanding leadership ability, she recognized that by offering them this recognition their loyalty to her would be ensured.

Of course, there was no way she would ever let either one of them have even the least amount of power. There was a hierarchy in the house that no one but she was aware of. Only one person held the power, and it wasn't even her. Every bit of power belonged to Horace. She simply did as he directed. She was the only one who even knew of his existence, and she would never take the chance of any of them coming between him and herself.

"You will use these skulls to bring me your most intimate offering. I will meet here with each of you individually when you have filled your skull within two inches from the top with your own menstrual blood. Whoever comes to me first will become the second in command of the Sisterhood of the Zodiac. You will use that offering to paint your astrological sign within the circle, as I have done. When this is done your test will be complete.

Go now, my true sisters. When we meet in this room once again and you complete your tasks we will become more than mere mortal sisters. We will mix our souls with the blood of our female bodies, making us greater than any who have come before us."

With that she ushered them out of the room. She wanted to laugh as she watched them carry the skulls in their hands as if they were about to use them to partake in a holy act.

What idiots they were. What sheep!

Chapter 25

Little by little the house became emptied of its more valuable antiques as Aries made additional trips out of town. Always following Horace's instructions, she continued searching for more girls to fill out the Zodiac. It was not easy to find girls who suited his stringent criteria. She was anxious to fill out the Zodiac, but realized finding the right candidates was more important than how long it took her to complete her task.

The first two times, when she returned with a fat wallet but no new girls, she'd worried what Horace's reaction to her failure would be. Surprisingly, rather than being angry he appeared to approve. After her second fruitless search he had actually given her one of his special treats, an extraordinarily intense orgasm. Afterwards, as she lay in the center of his circle, every ounce of energy drained from her body, he began to whisper what could only be described as his perception of pillow talk.

"You are part of me, my Aries," he whispered, "as I am all of you. When you make your choices, it is I who make them. The women you bring to me are of my choosing, not yours. I honor your willingness to bring me only those I show to you. This is how it is and how it must always be."

And then he entered even deeper into her mind. Now he was showing her in exquisite detail what she was to do next. As he filled her thoughts she felt her eyes drift shut. Flickering lights from the candles faded from her view as her lids closed.

She saw herself sitting in the main room downstairs, the room she shared each evening with all of the Sisterhood. As if in a vision, she saw girls she had already brought into the Zodiac, as well as some she had yet to procure. The girls were sitting or lying about the room, each one with her eyes closed. The only sound to be heard was the quiet droning of her own voice.

She knew instinctively what was happening. The night was not a night for listening to music and smoking pot, it was a night of soul traveling. She was in the middle of leading them through an LSD journey. It was something she had done back in the days when she had dabbled in what was being called the 'New Awakening.' But when she'd done it before, it had always been a one-on-one experience. She had never even considered herself capable of using her skills as a means of controlling so many minds. Only Horace could have given her such power.

The very next morning she made another trip to the Bay Area. She took more valuables with her, this time as a way to finance Horace's newest scheme rather than to add to the Sisterhood's coffers. To accomplish what Horace asked, she would need plenty of really good acid, which did not come cheap and she worried if she would still be able to hook up with one of her former suppliers. She'd been gone from the scene for nearly a year.

But, as ever, she had no problem accomplishing her objective. Horace was in control, not her. With him leading her, she knew she would never fail to fulfill his demands.

Her second goal for the trip was to fill out the membership of the Zodiac. Whereas, in her recent sojourns to the big cities she had been unable to find suitable members, on this trip they seemed to come to her as gifts from above.

One by one they came to her until she had filled the complete Zodiac with only one exception - Pisces. Aries extended her stay an entire day longer than she'd planned, hoping Pisces would come to her, but she finally heard Horace's voice telling her to come back to him, that they had been apart too long.

* * *

The scene was just as Horace had shown her it would be. She was sitting comfortably on a huge pillow in the middle of the room. The rest of the Sisterhood ranged throughout the combined living and dining rooms, all of them sitting quietly with their eyes closed, all listening intently to her voice.

Although many proponents of acid liked to use music during their trips, Aries preferred that her voice be all her travelers heard. Her words, or rather Horace's words, must be all that entered their minds during this time of altered awareness. She spoke softly, letting her words float upon the still air that filled the room.

She led them gently at first, talking them into seeing and hearing the best part of what the mountains offered - the sweet sounds of the river, the wind as it whispered in the trees. She reminded them how peaceful the sounds were, how comforting. Then, slowly yet inexorably, she made the sounds warp from peaceful to threatening, then into a thing beyond frightening.

"I will save you," she called to them over the roaring of the wind and the river that filled their minds. "Reach out your hand and I will take it." One by one each girl did as she was directed. Stepping from one girl to another, Aries touched each proffered hand, uttering soothing sounds and saying, "With my touch you are safe, but only with my touch.

"Still keeping your eyes closed, I want you to 'see' this room where we sit each night. Look around you. See the saris at the windows, the pillows, the chairs. See the colors of your happiness. You have never been as happy as you are at this very moment. This is the most important place in your entire life. You will do anything to keep this space, and the Sisterhood that occupies it, sacred.

"Now you are hearing voices from outside our walls. They are angry voices! They want what you have! They want to take it away from you. If you let them, they will force you out into the cold. Listen to them! Do you hear them pounding on the door? You want to get up and make them go away, but you can't. Your legs are melting! Look down at your legs. Do you see them melting?"

All of the girls were staring with horror at their legs. Some were trying unsuccessfully to move them, while others were reaching for them as if they had to touch them in order to believe this terrible thing that was happening. Tears were streaming down Libra's face. Several others were screaming in terror.

"Quiet!" Aries shouted. "I can help you but only if you listen carefully to what I say."

It took a moment or two but eventually silence returned to the room.

"I've made all the bad people go away. If you do what I say I will make them stay away and never bother you again. But you must always do as I say, or they will come back and I may not be able to drive them off. Now, look! Your legs are back to what they should be. I have saved you. I will always save you as long as you remain a true Sister of the Zodiac."

When she finally calmed the girls, she began to play a recording of the soothing sounds of a sitar.

"Listen, my sisters. Let yourselves blend into the music, let it become part of who you are. As you listen you will allow

yourself to fall into a deep, relaxing sleep. Sleep, my darlings …
sleep."

She left them and went upstairs. Going to each girl's room, she stripped off a blanket which she took downstairs and covered each girl where she slumbered. Knowing that each person reacted in her own way to acid, she had no idea how long it would take for the effects of the drug to wear off each individual girl. She expected that one or two might actually wake up before morning, but if they slept the night through, at least they wouldn't wake up chilled. When they did wake to see that she had covered them with their own blankets, her gesture would be just one more way for her to plant the thought into their minds that she cared deeply for their well-being.

When she was through, she went to her own room. She had done as Horace directed. Now it was time for him to give her the satisfaction she had earned.

Chapter 26

EMILY

Emily Matthews sipped her breakfast coffee on the deck Jim had just recently finished adding to their house. It was her favorite time of day during the summer, when there was still a nip to the morning air but enough sunshine to promise a beautiful afternoon.

As was their custom, she had prepared Jim an early breakfast before he headed off to the office. He frequently came home for lunch, or she might join him downtown at one of the town's excellent restaurants. On this day she had suggested he come home to eat as she intended to spend most of the day working on getting the back yard ready for summer. It was a job that would take at least a full week to accomplish.

Five years had passed since they had moved into the house. They had spent the first four remodeling the house over, one room at a time, making it the home of their dreams.

Taking a sip of coffee, she opened the town's weekly paper, 'The Dunsmuir News,' and prepared to read the headlines. But, instead of reading, she found herself staring off into space.

Something didn't feel quite right. Something uncomfortable tugged at her brain. It felt like a memory wanted to get out, yet the harder she tried to find it, the deeper it hid from her. What could …?

Then it came to her. It wasn't a memory, it was a dream.

Several times over the past few weeks she had woken with what she could only describe as a lurking sense of unease. There was nothing unpleasant going on in her life that could account for it. She had a husband she loved with all of her heart and she knew loved her with the same intensity. They were not wealthy, yet they had everything either one of them had ever dreamed of - the home of their dreams, a wonderful circle of friends and his very successful medical practice.

With a smile so often seen on a woman who has just recently discovered that her wish to welcome her own child into the world was finally coming true, she placed her hands gently upon her abdomen. It was far too soon to find out if the child who slept deep within her womb was a boy or a girl, but whichever it was, she and Jim already loved it for simply being the living expression of their love for one another.

Ever since the pregnancy had been confirmed Emily felt as if she were walking on a cloud. Happiness surged through her like a rising ocean tide whenever she thought about holding her own little baby to her breast.

But now she felt her heart tighten with concern when she realized her strange mood was over-shadowing her joyous feelings.

If she was a person prone to depression, she would have placed her unease at that doorstep. But she was reasonably certain that what she was experiencing was one more expression of her psychic abilities.

Being psychic had often caused her to have uncomfortable insights into what might be coming to her friends or other acquaintances, but this, whatever it was, felt different. She felt her heart race as she thought she might be having an unwelcome premonition about this child. Without thinking what she was doing, she pressed her hands more firmly against her stomach.

Closing her eyes, she forced herself to take three deep breaths, holding each one to the count of three, then releasing it. *It's not the baby*, she told herself. *I can't read for myself or for anyone close to me.* Taking three more deep breaths she began to feel her pulse slow. Relief swept through her when her new prospective mom emotions lost their grip.

The only thing she could think of that would have brought on such an unpleasant emotion would have been caused by her dreams. She often dreamed, occasionally several times in a single night. For the most part, they were fairly benign. But, every once in a while they were anything *but* benign. Sometimes even terrifying.

As far as dreams were concerned, Emily would have been very happy not to be psychic. Like everyone else on the planet, some of her dreams were fun, but a whole lot of others were scary. The problem was there was no way for her to tell which dreams were prophecies and which ones were just plain old ordinary dreams. She had lost count of the number of times she'd called her mother the day after a bad dream to inquire about the health of family members. Fortunately, the news had always been positive, yet she feared it might not always be.

Suddenly she knew the cause of her depression. The familiar sense of dread that had been troubling her became more intense as she recalled the dream that had come to her just moments before she awoke that morning. Her heart raced as she recalled it from the very beginning to the heartbreaking end.

In her dream she had been aware that she was in her bed, sound asleep, but as she lay there, unable to move or resist, Ada's spirit came to her. She was only a vaporous image at first, floating above the floor at the foot of her bed. Emily remembered trying to call out, but found that no matter how hard she tried to scream, she could make no sound, as if her vocal chords were paralyzed.

"Emily …" It was more as if she could feel her name being called than hear it. "Emily, dear, please listen to me."

The figure was becoming clearer now as it gathered more energy, coming closer to her. The body of the apparition began to disappear, until all that remained was a face, Ada's face.

Emily's fear turned to joy. It was Ada! How wonderful! Oh, how she had missed her old friend.

"Oh, Ada, I've missed you so much."

Suddenly it occurred to Emily that Ada might not realize she had died. She certainly didn't appear to be any different than when she was alive. Maybe she should tell her. But then, if she told Ada she was dead, it might spoil their visit.

She battled with herself for a few moments about the pros and cons of giving her old friend the sad news, but in the end she decided it was only right that her friend should know the truth.

"Ada, sweetie, you died."

"Oh, I know that," Ada replied with her familiar sweet smile. "It's not important. But what I came to tell you is. He's there, Emily … Horace, he's still there."

As she said those words, the smile on Ada's face disappeared and was replaced by the saddest expression Emily had ever seen.

"You have to go back to the house, Emily. You have to save them …"

And then she was gone, at least Emily couldn't remember there being any more to the dream. But what she did remember was almost more than she could bear.

Now, sitting in the coolness of the early morning, she couldn't fight off a sense of lingering sadness. So many emotions surrounded her memories of Ada, many of them wonderful, yet also so many sad ones. But at that moment the primary emotion she was experiencing was pure, unadulterated anger.

Go back to that horror palace? Not likely! She'd spent the past five years struggling to forget she'd ever set foot in that awful house. Why the hell did she have to start dreaming about her old friend now? And why the hell had her twisted subconscious mind have to come up with a dream about Ada?

Chapter 27

ARIES

Cancer's job at the bank was turning out to be very useful, even beyond the paycheck she handed over to Aries twice a month. More valuable than mere money was all of the information she picked up by interacting with her customers. One piece of information that intrigued Aries the most was the fact that the renowned Hearst family not only owned San Simeon, the famous mansion on California's central coast, they also owned a compound of homes, locally dubbed the 'other Hearst castles,' in a secluded area not far from the nearby city of McCloud.

When Cancer first mentioned the Hearst holdings so close to Dunsmuir, Aries had figured the story was one more example of how locals like to regale out-of-towners with their tall tales. Nowhere within the borders of Siskiyou County could there possibly be anything that came close to something that would interest people as rich as the Hearst's. However, after making some discreet inquiries, she discovered that Cancer's story was absolutely true: Not only did the Hearst family have holdings in Siskiyou County, the compound was no more than thirty miles from Dunsmuir.

The information she was able to glean without attracting too much attention was that it was a compound which was officially known as 'Wyntoon.' It was fully enclosed, except for where the boundary ran along the McCloud river, and consisted of several magnificent mansions. It was rumored that if a person did not have permission to enter it there was virtually no way they would be able to find a way in. Aries took that last bit of information as a challenge. If and when she decided she wanted to enter it, she would.

What intrigued Aries most about the Hearst compound was not the buildings themselves, but rather who she heard came to stay in them. Ever since she'd come to Dunsmuir she'd been planning on doing something that would make her and the Sisterhood more infamous than Charlie Manson and his gang. To accomplish that, not only would she need to do something far more horrendous than Charlie and his gang of nitwits had done, but her victims would have to be even more famous than his.

With Horace's guidance she felt she was making good progress in preparing the Sisters to do whatever she asked of them, even to the point of murder, but if she were to gain the sort of infamy she was craving, the Sisters would have to be willing to do something really awful, like kill a bunch of kids or something.

If what she had learned about the visitors to Wyntoon was correct, she need look no further. The kind of people who came to visit McCloud's Hearst compound might be exactly what she was looking for.

If she was going to target the Hearst camp, she needed to find someone who knew which guests were going to be there and codes, the layout, and the staff count. In short, she needed to find someone who worked there but, for whatever reason, hated his or her employer. Once again, she turned to Cancer.

Horace had done well when he told Aries to bring Cancer into the Sisterhood. She was in the perfect spot to gather the sort of information Aries needed and she had absolutely no compunction about sharing it with Aries. The local bank was not only the place most of the residents placed their money, it was also where people liked to visit as they stood in line waiting for their turn at the tellers. Cancer, with her friendly smile and willingness to listen, was the sort of person others felt comfortable visiting with, often telling secrets of their own and others' personal lives. After finishing their business with her, they left her with smiles on their lips, pleased at having been gifted with the new girl's time and sweet personality, never realizing they had left her with information that would one day make the name of their sleepy little town infamous.

Aries was astonished to learn that not only were film stars guests of the Hearst family, it was not at all unusual for state, and even federal, politicians to come up for a few days. When she heard a few of the names of famous senators, and even of a Supreme Court Justice, being mentioned as guests at the compound, she realized she had found what she called her "honey pot." After that it was simply a matter of getting the Sisters ready for the task, then waiting for the person or persons who would bring her the most press coverage.

"What we really need is to find a way to get more specific information," she told Cancer one night when Aries had invited her into her room. It was the one place in the mortuary where she could be certain they would not be overheard. It wasn't that she didn't trust any of the other Sisters, but rather that what she was planning was of a need-to-know nature. When the time came for action everyone would be thoroughly trained and ready to carry out her orders. But, until that day, each girl need know only her own part of the plan.

"I want you to find me someone who works at the Hearst compound. From what you've told me, the place is so huge there must be a team of people needed to keep it running. Those employees have to live somewhere. I can't imagine they all live on site. If we can find a few who live here in Dunsmuir, we ought to be able to find one or two who can give us the information we need."

A satisfied, 'I'm way ahead of you' smile spread across Cancer's face. "I think I already know the perfect guy. This guy, Jeff Withers, was in the bank a couple of days ago, all worried about how he was going to find someone who could help care for his crippled wife. He's the head grounds keeper at the Hearst place, so he's away from home a lot. His wife's in a wheelchair and needs a lot of help. The thing is, the lady who takes care of her is getting married in a couple of weeks and is moving down to Redding. They need someone ASAP, so the new gal can get trained and all. It's not a very complicated job - nothing that takes any special training. What they're looking for is someone the wife will enjoy having around, you know, someone young enough and strong enough to help her to the toilet and get her dressed in the morning, stuff like that. I was thinking maybe Scorpio might be able to do it."

Aries didn't say anything. She just sat there, nodding her head in agreement.

"I can ask Jeff if he wants to meet Scorpio, if you want. He seemed like he was really anxious to get Marie, that's his wife, taken care of."

"Let's do it," Aries responded, not even considering the need to ask Scorpio if she would be interested in the job. Being a member of the Sisterhood meant she would take whatever job Aries set up for her. Nor did she worry that the Withers might not want to hire Scorpio. If she had learned only one thing since embarking on this wild journey, it was that every step she took had been orchestrated by Horace. And Horace was never denied.

* * *

The secret meetings up in Aries' room were becoming more frequent now. First Aquarius, then Libra, arrived at her door at midnight, each holding glass skulls containing menstrual blood. After each presentation, Aries directed the presenter to dip her fingers in the blood. Using the blood like paint, she would then draw the outline of their own Zodiac sign within the Circle of the Sisterhood.

Because she was the first to return her skull, Aquarius was given the title of 'Second Sister.' Unknown to her, it was a title that actually represented nothing. True, Aries, as the 'First Sister', was the head of the Sisterhood, but there would never be a time when a Second Sister would have even the least amount of authority. It had always been Aries, and so it would stay all the way to the glorious end.

Even before the first two Sisters presented their sacrificial blood, the next two were called to Aries room for the first step of their inauguration. Aries was pleased to note that the tributes each one presented at their next meeting reflected the progress she made with them during the evening mind control sessions.

Gemini brought her a twelve inch chef's knife, so sharp it could cut paper as it floated in mid-air.

Cancer's contribution to the Sisterhood's growing arsenal was a hatchet. The eager glow Aries saw in the woman's eyes as she held the offering before her spoke volumes. If she were to ever choose a true Second Sister, it would be this woman. This was a woman who had the hungry look of a born killer in her eyes. She was exactly the person Aries wanted at her side on the day of society's reckoning.

Aries had still not found her Pisces. Although the fact that the Zodiac was not complete did not seem to worry Horace, it still troubled her. Deep in her bones she believed the circle must be complete if she, as the leader of the Sisterhood of the Zodiac, was to achieve her highest goal.

Chapter 28

NANCY

Nancy loved her new job. Marie was the sweetest woman in the world. And her husband, Jeff, was just the kind of man she would have chosen as a father if she'd been given the opportunity. Marie's last two caretakers had been older women. When they had been hired, Jeff believed they were better suited to care for his wife needs than a younger would have been. But when Nancy stood in their living room, fielding question after question without flinching, yet still appearing as vulnerable as a newborn kitten, both husband and wife found themselves thoroughly smitten. When she was offered the job she was beside herself with happiness. Her joy would have been complete if she had not been tasked by Aries to do something she knew without a doubt would cause her to be fired by her new employers if they ever found out.

Just two nights before her job interview Nancy attended her first Sisterhood inauguration meeting with Aries. She left Aries' room filled with a combination of joy and distress. It wasn't as if she hadn't known the meeting was coming: She'd heard bits and pieces of gossip from the other girls of what a person must do to become a full-fledged member of the Sisterhood; she knew it was a two-step process, but what those steps entailed was never revealed. The secrecy of it all made it all the more exciting when she received her call.

She had come away from it with a driving need to steal. The thought was with her always, reminding her constantly that until she brought something back to Aries, something that could do deadly harm to another human being, she would be but a probationer at the mansion.

She had never known such peace and happiness as she'd found while living with the Sisterhood. She would do anything to make her position there permanent. She wanted - no, she needed - to find the perfect weapon, a weapon so wonderful even Aries would be impressed.

The one place she could not steal from was the home of her new employers. When she was with the Withers she felt different, more like what she believed a normal person might feel. Thoughts of thievery did not belong anywhere near their house, especially thoughts of stealing a weapon that could cause another person's death!

Sometimes she had the sensation of being two people, one who hated the whole world except for the Sisterhood and another who, when she was with the Withers, felt what it must be like to be loved. Each night as she lay in her bed back at the mansion the two parts would do battle with one another, each trying to overwhelm the other. She'd lived with cruelty and hatred for so many years they were the emotions that felt normal to her. But, as she began to allow herself to plan how and from whom she would steal her weapon, the goodness of the Withers came into her heart.

The constant fight between good and evil kept her awake night after night, until one night she decided she'd had enough. She climbed out of bed, determined that this was when she would fulfill Aries' request. Without giving herself time to think of what she was doing, she pulled on a pair of dark blue jeans and a black hoodie, then slipped quietly out of the house. Her only burglary tool was a credit card, but she figured it would be all she needed if she was lucky enough to find the right kind of door lock.

It took her three tries before she found a house with a lock she could open with her credit card.

She felt totally out of her league when it came to stealing weapons, but the actual deed turned out to be easier than she had hoped. Being a mountain town, many of its citizens were avid hunters. Her hope was that she would be able to find a house like one she had seen on TV, where the hunter always hung his rifle or shotgun on a rack over the fireplace. With that in mind, she passed up any house that did not have a chimney.

After entering the living room of the first house, she realized it was a house that was not at all likely to have a gun. Everywhere she looked all she could see were toys. As she pointed her penlight first around the kitchen, and then the living room, she did not see one thing that looked the least bit masculine. The one place she had hoped to find a gun, the mantelpiece, was littered with fancy little statues. She slipped out of the house as quietly as she had entered.

It took her two more tries before she finally found what she needed. There, on a rack over the fireplace, just exactly as she had pictured it, was as pretty a rifle as she'd ever seen, even on TV. And, wonders of all wonders, lying on the mantelpiece directly below the rifle was what looked to be an antique pistol. She quickly slipped the pistol into the deep pocket of the hoodie and lifted the rifle down from the rack. Being careful to not bang the rifle against anything on her way out, she tiptoed back through the kitchen and made her exit.

On the way back to the mansion Nancy's soul once again did battle. Puffed up with adrenalin, exhilaration warred with guilt. The sense of exhilaration won out.

Not wanting to leave the two weapons in her room, she decided to wake Aries and chance being reprimanded.

Apparently she had wakened Aries from a deep sleep if the woman's appearance was any indication. But as soon as she saw what the young girl was holding in her hands, Aries quickly ushered her into her room. Within fifteen minutes Nancy was walking out of the room, holding a small glass skull in her hands.

Before the door closed, all of Aries' attention was riveted to the gifts she had just been given. They weren't simply guns, they were valuable antique guns. Once again she saw the hand of Horace at work.

* * *

"She made you do *what*?" Eddy was standing at the breakfast table, pouring coffee for the two of them. So shocked at what he had just heard he completely forgot what he was doing until coffee overflowed the mug he was filling and began dripping on the floor at his feet.

"Hey! Watch it!" Nancy yelled as she jumped back out of the way of the steaming liquid. "It's not that big a deal," she continued in her regular voice as she reached for the roll of paper towels and began soaking up the spilled coffee. "It's not like she's making us commit a serious crime or anything."

"*Serious?* You don't call breaking and entering, stealing stuff, stealing *guns, serious?*"

"Well, if you put it like that …"

"Yes, I *put it like that!* You were a God-damned burglar! Do you realize how much time they would give you if you got caught?"

"But I didn't get caught, did I?"

"And you stole two God-damned guns? Are you crazy?" Before she could answer, Eddy continued. "What the hell does she want guns for, anyway? I suppose she's going to get you bunch of idiots to rob a bank next!"

Rather than answer him, Nancy simply stood there, looking everywhere but at him.

"Oh, my God," he whispered as he slowly sat down at the kitchen table. When she saw the color leave his face, Nancy knew she had said more than she should have. "It's not a bank. It's something worse, isn't it?"

"You know I can't tell you that. I've said too much already. If any of the Sisterhood found out I've been talking to you ..."

His face faded to an even lighter shade of white.

"Please, don't say anything!" she pleaded. "Please?"

He sat there for a moment, gazing at her with so much pain in his eyes she thought she might end up bawling right there in front of him. She hated admitting it even to herself, but what had been happening with the Sisterhood lately had been worrying her. She'd always managed to ignore her concerns when she was with everyone else, but Eddy's reaction was starting to make her take a second look.

Well, damn it, she didn't want to take a second look. She didn't want to lose Eddy, but even more she didn't want to lose the Sisterhood. It was everything to her.

"I gotta get to work," she mumbled as she turned to leave. "I didn't mean any of that stuff I was telling you. I just wanted to see how you would take it, you know? It was all a big joke. Please don't say anything, okay? Please?"

He didn't answer her. He simply sat there at the kitchen table, watching her leave. He knew he should say something to someone, but who? Being the wimp he'd turned into, he knew he wouldn't do a damned thing. What the hell had he gotten himself into?

Chapter 29

Nancy felt like she'd been walking around with a pound of angry bees in her stomach ever since she'd told Eddy about the gun thing. Part of the time she was pissed off at how he reacted. After all, he wasn't exactly the most standup guy himself. Okay, so he didn't do any breaking and entering, like she and the other girls had, but it wasn't like he never broke the law, either. The last time she looked, it was still against the law to smoke dope in the state of California. He didn't seem to mind doing that just about every day of his life.

And who was he to preach morals to her? Wasn't he the guy that slept with a different woman every night? If he'd been a female acting like that, he'd been called a whole lot of dirty words and he would have been guilty of every single one of them. Was there such a thing as a 'guy-whore,' she wondered?

But as soon as she'd think things like that about Eddy, those damned old bees would suddenly start buzzing around in her tummy even worse than before. Eddy was the best friend she'd ever had. Hell, who was she kidding? He was the *only* friend she'd ever had. He hadn't taken her to bed like he'd every right to do back when she'd first come to the mansion. It hadn't been because he didn't like her, either - it was because he *did* like her. At least that's what he'd told her. Had she been some kind of fool to believe him?

Now she'd gone and made him mad at her. No, not so much at her; it was more like he was mad at Aries for telling her to go steal that stuff. If she'd only kept her damned mouth shut.

The thing was, when she thought about what Eddy said, she knew he was right. Why did Aries want all those guns and stuff? Nancy knew she hadn't been around as much as she'd thought she had, but she was pretty sure the things Aries was getting her and the other Sisters to do didn't make a lot of sense. That was unless, like Eddy said, she wanted the Sisterhood to go out and rob a bank or something.

More bees buzzed in her belly when she realized Eddy might not be too far off. If she was being completely truthful with herself, she had to admit robbing a bank might not actually be as bad as what Aries was actually planning. She didn't want to think what could be worse than robbing a bank, but all of Aries' talk about upping old Charlie Manson didn't make the bees quiet down one bit.

She'd never taken Aries serious when she talked about the Manson family - after all, who would? - But now ...

* * *

Nancy managed to put thoughts about bank robberies and what could be worse as she made her way to Aries' room at midnight several days later. She was cradling what she thought might be the most disgusting thing she'd ever seen, a glass skull which held her own menstrual blood. She didn't want to think about the blood, nor how she'd gone about collecting it. Everything about it was so repulsive just thinking about it made her want to gag. She was really getting tired of some of the things Aries was making her do.

She tapped lightly at Aries' bedroom door. It was opened immediately. Standing just inside the door was Aries, who stepped back and gestured for the girl to enter.

"Welcome, Scorpio. I see you have brought your sacred offering to the Sisterhood."

Nancy, not being able to think of an appropriate response to Aries' comment, simply stood there gazing at the candles and the Zodiac circle on the floor.

Following Aries' directions she then did what she could only think of as an even more disgusting thing than what she'd already done. She dipped her fingers into the semi-coagulated blood and carefully etched the image of a scorpion on the inside of the circle.

"You may rise now, Scorpio, Sister of the Zodiac," Aries said as she walked toward her.

When Nancy had risen and stood before Aries, the leader of the Sisterhood reached out with both hands and clasped the younger woman by the shoulders. Holding her firmly, she leaned toward her and kissed her directly on the mouth.

Nancy felt she might die of humiliation when she felt the tip of Aries' tongue try to enter her mouth. *What the hell?*

Aries stepped back, a small, knowing smile on her face. "Scorpio, my sweet, I must tell you. You are the most beautiful woman I have ever kissed."

The words, "Thank you," tumbled out of Nancy's mouth, to her even greater embarrassment. What she was actually thinking was *ick! ick! ick!* But she managed to keep herself from saying it. Instead, she turned as quickly as she could and ran to her own room, where she locked the door then placed a chair under the doorknob.

She didn't hear the sound of Aries' laughter following her down the hallway, nor did she hear the sound of Horace's angry voice shouting, "I told you, no virgins!"

* * *

Aries' first reaction to Horace's tirade was complete shock. What was Horace talking about? He couldn't be talking about Scorpio. She remembered quite clearly the girl's reaction when she asked her if she was a virgin. It couldn't have been more obvious that the girl's only concern was that she would not be welcome at the mansion if she was a virgin.

And then there was Eddy. Hadn't he been asking for Scorpios services more often than any of the other girls? She knew

Eddy's sexual appetites well enough to know he would never be satisfied with a platonic relationship.

"Who're you talking about, Horace? I've never brought a virgin into the house. I never would!"

"She's a lying little bitch, just like that damned wife of mine. Virgins! They're all nothing more than lying, sniveling bitches. I won't have one in my house! If you won't get rid of her, I will. And I promise you, if I have to do it, I'll take every damned one of you with her, straight to hell."

He left her standing in the center of the room, shaking with anger and fear.

* * *

Nancy went to work the next morning as if nothing unusual had happened, but knowing in her heart she would never return to the mortuary. She didn't know how she was going to do it, but she did know she had to put as much space between Aries and herself as possible. When her mother threw her out of the house she had been willing to do a lot of things just to survive, but being a lesbian's lover was not one of them.

She couldn't explain it: Though she'd been willing to whore herself out, she'd figured she'd be doing it with guys, not girls, She'd even been willing to break into people's houses and steal from them, even steal weapons that she was beginning to believe might actually be used to kill people. It made her sick to her stomach to realize she'd been willing to do all those things. Now she couldn't help wondering, what kind of person was she that the only thing she backed away from was something as innocuous as getting kissed by another woman?

By the time she reached the Withers' house she had finally managed to untangle her thoughts. It wasn't just the one thing that bothered her. It was all the things she'd been asked to do, things that were not part of who she was. Oh, who was she kidding? It was all the things she had already done. The kiss had simply been the one thing … what did people call it? The straw that broke the camel's back. It was just one thing too much. Thank God it hadn't taken robbing a bank, or even worse, murdering someone, to wake her up to what was happening.

When she arrived at the Withers' house the first thing she did was to announce she was leaving town, so she would no longer be able to work for them. The tears that welled up in her eyes took her by surprise. She was not someone who cried easily, but the thought of leaving Marie and Jeff hit her in the heart.

"But *why?*" Marie had cried. "Do you need more money?"

"No, no, it isn't that. It's just …" There was no way she could tell Marie the truth about who she really was and the things she had done.

"Do you have another job?"

"Oh, Marie, I wouldn't leave you for something like that. I love you guys, I really do. This is the best job I've ever had."

"Then why leave? Did something happen over at the place you live? You know, if you can't stay there, you can stay with us. We have that empty guest room. We'd love it if you would stay here."

Nancy knew Marie's suggestion could not be a permanent solution, but it might work for the time-being. She was scared to death about what Aries might do to her, but maybe she would be safe with the Withers, at least for a little while.

Chapter 30

ARIES

Aries' furor had not diminished one iota when she awoke the next morning. It took all of her willpower to keep from thundering up the stairs to Eddy's room and tearing him to hell and back. How dare he deceive her like that?

And talk about deception! That lying little bitch, Scorpion! When she got hold of her she'd kill her with her bare hands.

The past night had been one long nightmare. She'd tried for hours to placate Horace's wrath, all to no avail. This morning had been the first time since she had discovered his essence that he'd refused to satisfy her sexual needs.

Her first instinct when she realized how badly she had failed Horace had been to find the damned lying bitch and beat the last breath from her body. When she was through with her she'd do the same to Eddy, that worthless piece of shit. What the hell had he been thinking, keeping information like that a secret? Secrets, other than her own, were not allowed in the Sisterhood! When you let the stupid sheep keep secrets, you lost control. Which was something she would never allow. Who the hell did he think he was?

She was halfway up the stairs to his apartment when common sense stopped her. Alright, so he'd kept a secret from her. The fact that she knew about it was a secret she needed to keep from him. She hadn't lost control, she had only gained more. She turned around and descended to the first floor.

She'd always wondered why Horace insisted that she bring him only non-virgins. The only reason she could think of was that he wanted women who had experienced enough of life to be open to his desires. Now she knew there was far more to the virgin thing than she had ever imagined. She also knew that bringing him a virgin was something she would never, ever, do again. And, she also knew she would have to find some other way to determine a girl's sexual experience than by sending her to Eddy.

* * *

The breakfast table was one girl short that morning, Aries noted as she sat down at her place at the head of the table. "Did Scorpio already leave for work?" she asked as she scooped scrambled eggs onto her plate.

"I guess so," Libra replied as she placed a bacon-loaded platter on the table. "She must have left really early, 'cuz I didn't see her, even though I was up by six. Maybe she had to get to work early or something."

Libra's answer seemed possible to Aries. There had been a couple of days before when Jeff had asked Scorpio to come in early because he was scheduled for a couple extra hours. He always tried to go in early rather to come home late.

She was not overly concerned that something might be wrong until Scorpio had not returned in time for dinner. When she still hadn't come home by the time they had all taken their places in the living room later that evening, Aries began to suspect she might have yet another problem on her hands.

After checking Scorpio's room the next morning, only to discover the girl had still not returned, Aries decided she had to do something. She waited until the middle of the morning before going to the Withers' home. She felt like a parent checking up on her wayward daughter as she waited for the door to be opened.

She'd worked too hard molding the Sisters into empty-headed tools to let one simple-minded girl screw up everything. It would have been bad enough if Libra or Aquarius had decided to run off - the work they did at the house could be accomplished by just about anyone.

Although Horace demanded that Aries get rid of her, Scorpio was the Sister who held the key to everything. Aries needed someone in the Withers' house, someone Jeff would trust. Not just with the care of his wife but with the secrets he carried in his head. If Aries could not find out who was coming to the

Hearst place, and when they would be there, there was virtually no way she could reach her goal. It boiled down to a simple equation, *no Scorpio = no massacre* and *no massacre = no fame.* Which was an absolutely unacceptable equation. She'd come this far; she was not about to give up. After she got Scorpio back she'd figure out how she was going to deal with Horace.

Scorpio answered Aries' knock. The girl stood there, the door only partially opened, a very wary expression on her face.

"Would it be alright if I came in? We need to talk."

Aries could hear the TV playing one of the early morning talk shows.

"I don't know. I'm kind'a busy right now."

Aries managed a tight smile as her mind searched for whatever words she needed to get the stupid girl back into the fold.

"We really do need to talk, Scorpio. Couldn't I come in for just a minute?"

Rather than invite her in, Nancy stepped onto the porch, closing the door behind her. Realizing this was the best chance she was going to get, Aries said, "I know you're upset about something, Scorpio, but I'm sure whatever's bothering you is nothing that can't be worked out. Please, tell me what's wrong."

Nancy stood still for a moment. Finally, she blurted out, "I'm no lesbian!"

"Oh, is that all? Of course you're not a lesbian, neither am I! It was the kiss, right?"

"And the tongue!"

"Oh, sweetheart, that was only part of the ritual. It didn't mean anything."

"And I don't want to be any dumb burglar, either. What're you doing, collecting knives and guns and stuff?"

"None of that means anything. It's all just part of going through an initiation into a secret society. That kind of thing happens all the time. You know, in all kinds of regular organizations. You just don't hear about it because it's all kept secret. You're done with it now."

"I'm not going to have to do any more criminal stuff?"

"No! I promise you really and truly are done with doing any more criminal stuff."

"But I don't see why I had to do that stuff in the first place. I could'a gotten in a lot of trouble if I'd got caught."

"Well, that's true. I can't deny it. Maybe I did go a bit overboard when I made up the rituals. I just wanted to make sure we didn't get any members in the Sisterhood who weren't completely committed to being part of us. Hey, I tell you what. If you don't like all that stuff, from now on no one will ever have to do it again. Now that you've brought it to my attention that what we were doing really could get someone in trouble, I'm sorry I ever thought it was such a good idea."

"You mean it?"

"I do! Cross my heart and hope to die," Aries said as she made a backward sign of the cross, using her left hand, "I promise to never ask any of the Sisters to steal one more thing." It was a promise that would not be hard to keep, since all of the Sisters had already passed that part of their initiation. But none of that mattered anyway, since Aries never made a promise she bothered to keep. "Now, will you please come back to us? You really are missed, you know."

Releasing a huge sigh of relief, Nancy smiled her agreement. "I'll be back for dinner, okay?"

"Okay it is!"

Aries left, determined to never let Scorpio suspect her true mission.

Chapter 31

For the most part everything went along as usual at the mansion for the next three weeks. The only difference from what life had been before Scorpio agreed to return was her absence at the evening gatherings in the living room. It had never been discussed but she'd decided that doing dope, and whatever else it was Aries was giving the Sisters, was not something she wanted to do.

It irritated Aries that any of the girls seemed to think they could do whatever they pleased while still living at the mansion, but since it was Scorpio, she decided to let it go. If pushed too hard she knew the girl would leave for good the next time. If that happened Aries would have no choice: She would have to find her, and this time rather than bringing her back, she would have to be sure the girl would be unable to give any of the Sisterhood's secrets away. She had never actually killed anyone before, but knew in her heart that if Horace told her to, she would do it without a second thought. She was just relieved that none of the other girls appeared to be interested in following Scorpio's lead.

Aries was careful to keep an eye on the girl, noting how much time she and Eddy spent together, wondering what it was he found so interesting that it kept him meeting with her far more frequently than with any of the others. In Aries mind

Scorpio had turned into an enemy. If she hadn't needed the information Scorpio was able to provide, she would have been happy to get rid of her permanently.

In the meantime, all Aries could do was wait. She knew the moment she so desperately longed for would eventually come, but when? The waiting was horrible, yet never as horrible as what she planned for her future victims, whoever they turned out to be. She knew where it would happen; what she didn't know was who or when. In the meantime each day passed slowly as she waited for more information.

The information, when it did come, came to her in bits and pieces. And, surprisingly, it did not come from Scorpio.

The first inkling she had that the time for action was nearing was when Cancer came to her with the very interesting news that she had met a man who had once worked for the Hearst Estate but had recently been fired. According to him he was completely innocent of their charges. He had never stolen one thing from those "God-damned snobs." Not anything they would ever need, anyway. How was he supposed to know there were surveillance cameras hidden all over the place? As far as he was concerned the Hearsts were nothing more than a bunch of too-rich bastards who wanted to keep hard working guys like himself under their thumbs.

And as for their claim that he was drinking on the job, what the hell were they talking about? He'd never once taken even one sip of whiskey while he was working, and that was a God-damned fact! What he did on his lunch break and before he came to work was none of their damned business. They seemed to think just because he worked for them they had the right to tell him how to run his life.

The day John Severin came into the bank to cash his severance check he confided to Cancer how that "holier than thou Hearst bunch" had better watch their backs. He knew enough about them and how they ran those fancy damned mansions of theirs to get back at them whenever he felt like it. Nothing would make him happier than to see a couple of those damned "summer homes" of theirs go up in flames.

Cancer was very pleased to set him up for coffee with her very good friend Aries.

Aries kept her meetings with John all to herself. She noted the first time they met that he was the sort of braggart who couldn't get enough attention. All she had to do was to keep telling him how great he was and he'd tell her whatever she wanted to know about the Hearst family and their Wyntoon holdings.

Their first meeting was for coffee; their second was for dinner. By the end of that meeting he could hardly wait to take her for a boat ride down the river that skirted the Hearst property.

They went during the day the first time, then late at night the next. She wanted to see everything - how far back the buildings were from the river, the best places where a boat could land and be hidden. The entire time they were on the river he kept talking about burning the whole "damned place" down, while she studied every turn in the river and every other marker that could help her find her way back. After making the two excursions with him, she was certain once they reached their target, John's services would no longer be necessary.

"You know what, John? Between the two of us, and a few other people I know who hate the high and mighty Hearsts as much as you, I think we can do it."

"Do what?"

"Burn the place down!"

The expression she saw on the man's face by the moon's faint light was a mixture of shock and admiration. They were sitting in his boat, gliding quietly past the compound's forbidden property. Even in the dark it was not hard to see the many 'Private Property,' 'Do Not Enter,' 'No Trespassing on Penalty of the Law' signs.

"You'd do that?"

"You'd damn well better believe it. Are you in?" she asked, hoping to bring fresh flames to his hatred.

There was just the briefest of seconds before he responded with, "Hell yeah, I'm in."

Aries wanted to laugh out loud. She'd done it! She'd found what was probably the only person in the entire county who could get her in the compound and was dumb enough to actually do it. His services would be invaluable.

Of course, she'd have to kill him before the real slaughter began. After all, she wasn't about to let anyone believe he was part of her gang. Hell, if he wasn't the first one dead, everyone would think he was the leader of the Sisterhood, and that was something she would never allow. She would get her fame, all of it. No fool of a man was ever going to take it away from her.

* * *

It was just a couple of days after her second trip down the river with John when Aries noted once again that Scorpio was not at the table for breakfast. Her lips tightened at the thought that the stupid girl might have run off again.

"Where's Scorpio, does anyone know?" she asked, looking around the table at the other girls who all were busy eating.

"She had to leave early this morning," Libra answered. "She was up and out of here by six-thirty. She said Mr. Withers told her he's going to be working some long hours for the next few days. He said the Hearst family's coming up for Patty's birthday next week and his bosses want the whole place looking special.

Libra's statement caused Aries to almost drop the forkful of food.

"Patty Hearst?" she echoed, just to make sure.

"Yeah, I guess so. Scorpio said the kid was the big guy's granddaughter, so yeah, I guess it's her."

Aries forgot all about eating as she considered the enormity of what Libra had just said. So, the Hearst family was planning a birthday party for Patty. It was already the middle of February and the grounds were being prepared right now. That must mean the actual birthday must be coming up soon. If that was so, then dear, sweet rich-bitch Patty Hearst was a Pisces - the one astrological sign the Sisterhood was missing! Yes!

She rose slowly from the table, her mind too busy exploring all of the ramifications of what she had just learned to even think of something as trivial as food. Leaving the room without speaking, she headed directly to her room, and to Horace. Breakfast was the last thing she wanted as she let her imagination explore the possibilities.

Chapter 32

The implications of what she had just learned were overwhelming, so overwhelming in fact that Aries' mind was so full of excitement she did not even think to call Horace to be with her when she entered her room.

Patty, was her Pisces! She was the final link in the circle. If Patty became part of the Sisterhood, the circle of the Zodiac would be complete. Their power would be absolute. There would be nothing stopping the Sisterhood of the Zodiac from committing crimes so heinous history would never forget them. And the world would never forget Aries, the woman who conceived and directed the most infamous criminals in the annals of history. She would be the woman who had commanded the most vicious women ever known to mankind.

Her heart raced with excitement as she dialed John Severin's phone number.

Chapter 33

She'd already decided she would have to kill John Severin. Now, after spending two full days trying to get him sober, she was about as ready to do the act. The only thing keeping him alive was that she still needed his help.

After tomorrow night everything would change. The Sisterhood would have their Pisces and the worthless piece of humanity that called himself John Severin would be dead. That alone was all that allowed him to live one more day.

When she thought about how far she had come in the past year she could hardly believe her good fortune. Everything had gone way beyond what she could have ever imagined before she hooked up with Eddy. Although he wasn't worth a fuck, if it hadn't been for him she would never have come up with the idea of one-upping that piece of shit, Charlie Manson, and she would never have found Dunsmuir and the building that had become the foundation for the Sisterhood.

She couldn't keep from smiling when she thought of the one attribute the building possessed that would make her plan possible, the cement rooms that had once been the actual working part of the mortuary, the rooms where she would keep the Hearst heiress until she was convinced that being the final link in the Zodiac was her destiny.

Throughout Aries' life no one had ever considered her as someone worth even the smallest attention. The look she had so frequently seen in her parents' eyes told her what they thought of their child, that she was too dumb to bother with. But she wasn't dumb; quite the contrary. She saw and heard everything, keeping her own council, never letting anyone know how smart she was.

If she was so stupid, would she have known about 'Stockholm's Syndrome'? But she did know about it. She read, damn it! And she knew how she was going to use it to turn Patty Hearst into the most loyal member the Sisterhood of the Zodiac had ever seen.

* * *

Crouching down low to the earth, John motioned for Aries to join him. Spread out before them were several houses that to Aries all appeared to be mansions. Other than a couple of outdoor lights, the entire area lay in darkness. Not one window in any of the houses showed even a glimmer of light.

Aries had brought only Libra and Aquarius with her. This was the type of mission that could be ruined by having too many participants. She didn't need all of the Sisterhood, but she did need the most daring and the most clever. Libra and Aquarius both possessed those traits.

"Which house is she in?" Aries whispered in John's ear.

"That one there to the right, the one that has the balloons and streamers all over the yard. I guess they've had the kid's party already."

The word 'kid' struck an odd chord in Aries' brain; that and all the childish decorations.

"John, how old is Patty?" Aries whispered.

"Hell, I don't know. She's a kid!"

"Like, she's probably a virgin?"

"Yeah, I guess so. How the hell am I supposed to know? What do you think I am, a pervert?"

"No, John, I do not think you're a pervert. What I do think is you're a dead man."

Aries took the machete she had brought with her and, with one swift downward swing, severed his head from his body. With a swift kick, she pushed his body aside and motioned for Libra and Aquarius. Bemoaning the fact that she could kill him only once, she gestured for the Sisters to gather around her. "There's been a slight change of plans."

As if she were doing nothing more unusual than picking up trash, Aries reached down and picked up John's head by each ear and began walking toward the river. Glancing over her shoulder, she whispered to the other two girls, "Grab the arms of that piece of shit and help me get him down to the river."

Without giving Aries even the slightest glance of concern, Aquarius and Libra did as they were told.

Chapter 34

Aries prided herself on never losing control. Even during her hippy time, which for most were lost days and sometimes years, she always knew what she wanted and how to get it. But the debacle at Wyntoon had hit her hard. How could she have made so many stupid mistakes?

The answer to that question was all too obvious. She had become prideful, too full of herself to seek Horace's guidance. She'd told herself she had done it to please him, but now she saw the falsehood for what it was. She hadn't wanted to please Horace; she had gone ahead without consulting him because she wanted to prove she was stronger than him.

Her relationships with Scorpio and Eddy had gone from bad to worse. Although Scorpio continued to live and take most of her meals at the mortuary, the wedge between Aries and the girl had only become wider. Aires could not remember the last time the two of them had communicated on even the most superficial level. If it wasn't that the other girls would question Scorpio's absence, Aries would be all too happy to do to her what she had done to John. How she longed to feel her machete slice the girl's head from her body and watch it float down the river like a child's lost rubber ball!

And Eddy was no better. Once again she'd lost control. She couldn't remember the last time he asked her to refill his supply of pot. If she didn't know him better, she would believe he'd actually given up the stuff. She wondered if he had gone out on his own and found another supplier.

And it wasn't just the hash that worried her. Several of the girls had come to her complaining that he hadn't requested their services. Didn't he know part of their deal was that the sex wasn't just for his own enjoyment? The girls had needs which he was not satisfying.

Since Aries discovered how fully Horace was able to satisfy her own needs, she really hadn't paid much attention to Eddy's sexual life. For all she knew, he might have stopped using the girls weeks ago. Frankly, she didn't care who he fucked, or even if he'd given up fucking altogether, but considering his friendship with Scorpio and all the trouble the little bitch was causing, she realized the changes in Eddy might need to be looked into. One rebel in the crowd was one too many. She could not allow there to be two.

The problem was she had become so accustomed to allowing Horace to direct everything she did and said she'd forgotten she was the one in charge of the Sisterhood. He had become everything to her, the very center of her being. But ever since she made the stupid mistake of not checking into Patty Hearst's age and sexual status, her lover was no longer so attentive.

Oh, it wasn't as if he never came to her, he did, but not as often nor as satisfyingly as before. Night after night she offered herself to him, waiting for him, longing for him, but all too often when he came it was only to tantalize her with the knowledge of his presence while holding back his full essence.

Each night, after experiencing his cold presence, she would leave the room, walking the halls for hours. She rarely slept now. Nor did she eat. Coffee and weed were all that kept her going.

It wasn't long before the Sisters began to take notice of their leader's strange behavior. They became restless, fearful. She was the glue that held the Sisterhood together. What would they do without her? The Sisters came to her, each one trying in her own way to find a way to help keep the abyss they feared she was about to fall into at bay.

Libra and Aquarius prepared special meals for her. Cancer continued bringing her tidbits of information she thought might entice Aries out of her depression. Nothing seemed to work until Leo and Capricorn came to her with news that brought her back.

Chapter 35

Leo and Capricorn were the most recent girls to join the Sisterhood and, for a while, the most difficult for Aries to find employment for. Neither of them had even the least amount of work experience, which made it difficult for Aries to find them jobs either in Dunsmuir or Mt. Shasta. Both cities were short of employment opportunities so it was next to impossible to find work for such inexperienced girls.

Aries was beginning to think they would never be able to carry their portion of the financial load until she heard about a profitable, if not the most legal, business down south of Dunsmuir, in an area called Castella. It was close enough to Dunsmuir to be serviced by its post office, yet far enough from town to be out of the jurisdiction of the nearest law enforcement officials. It sat just south of the Siskiyou County border and at the very north edge of Shasta County. In other words, the tiny mountainous community was for all intents and purposes as wide open as the locals allowed it to be … which was as open as all get out.

When Babe Ruth was in his glory, it was said his favorite bar and brothel could both be found there. The days of the Babe's attendance were long gone now, but the entertainment facilities were still very popular with both locals who could afford their services as well as more than a few film and political celebrities.

The odd part of the thing was that most of the citizens of Dunsmuir were either unaware of the goings-on down there or, figuring that as long as it wasn't happening in the own town they preferred to look the other way.

The main business in Castella was its hotel, which contained Buck's Bar and a brothel. Food was also served at Buck's, but was not much of a draw. After all, if a man was drunk enough and fucked enough, who cared a rat's ass what the food tasted like?

Besides the hotel, there were several small stone cottages. A few of them were owned by gentlemen who preferred their entertainment to be of a more personal nature. Four of the cottages were maintained by the brothel for use by its more elite clients.

It was to the hotel that Aries brought Leo and Capricorn. She had no illusion that Leo, a rather drab girl, would ever be chosen to work in the better-paid position - that of a whore - but Capricorn was perfect for the job.

Capricorn was arguably the most beautiful of all the Sisters. She was tall - nearly 5'11" - slender and had legs that had been created solely to fulfill a man's erotic dreams. She wore her silky, auburn-colored hair in a page boy style. Her bangs were cut in a straight line above her brows, forming a frame for her almost perfect face. The hairstyle accentuated elegantly arched brows and emerald green eyes. A light sprinkling of freckles across her nose brought a fresh, youthful appearance to her peaches and cream complexion. Her sultry voice could give even the least masculine man the biggest hard-on he had ever experienced.

After one look at Capricorn, the brothel's Madam quickly installed her in Cabin #4, which made several of the other girls so angry they spent most of their off-time trying to come up with ways to disgrace the new kid on the block. Capricorn, for her part, realizing how much the cabin work was desired by all of the girls, suggested to the Madam that they take turns using it when she was off-duty.

In less than a week Capricorn endeared herself to customers and workers alike, just as Aries had instructed her. The money Capricorn brought to the Sisterhood was be good, but nothing compared to the value of the information about the influential guests she passed on to Aries.

Leo, while not being what anyone would call beautiful, turned out to be the most popular cocktail waitress Buck's Bar had ever known. It was not unusual for her to end her nightly shift with as much in tips as some of the girls who worked the hotel rooms earned. She was friendly, without being seductive; cute rather than beautiful. Her most appreciated attribute, to both her customers and Aries, was she that was the kind of girl people felt comfortable confiding in.

Chapter 36

Aries was so wrapped up in her misery over being neglected by Horace she failed to notice Scorpio's absence from the breakfast table until the third day had passed without her presence. The only reason she noticed it even then was that Libra made a comment about it.

"You'd think if a person was not going to eat with us they'd just say so. I wonder if anyone ever told Scorpio that it's just wrong to waste food."

"Something big must be coming up at Wyntoon," Aries commented to no one in particular as she ladled a large serving of scrambled eggs onto her plate.

"I can't remember Mr. Withers ever working so many overtime hours except when something big was coming up. You know, like that time when the Hearst family came up for Patty's birthday," Libra continued. "And even then he only had to work a couple of extra days. As much overtime as he's pulling down lately, they must be expecting someone real important."

Cancer set her coffee cup down as she turned to look at Aries. "I think she may be right. The last few days I've been noticing some of customers at the bank have been acting a little … oh, I don't know how to put it. It's like they're all excited about something. It's kind'a like there's a charge of electricity buzzing around town but no one wants to admit it."

For the first time in weeks, Aries gave her full attention to the Sisters. Her eyes widened in excitement as she asked Libra how long Scorpio had been going in early.

"She's only done it three times. But still …"

"Did she say anything about why?"

"No, not really," Libra answered. "She just said she needed to go take care of Marie, 'cuz Jeff was needed up at the compound."

Turning her attention back to Cancer, Aries asked, "Are there any weak links among your customers? You know, someone who puts being in the loop above keeping secrets?"

"I know of one lady like that but she hasn't been in lately."

"Could you give her a call? Maybe ask her out for coffee?"

"I don't know …"

"If she's as much a gossip as you've made her seem, I'd think it would be worth trying to contact her personally. She's probably one of those women who love gossip so much she'd be happy for any opportunity to share her news."

"I've been noticing something about my customers at the bar, now that you mention it," Leo offered. "Several of my regulars work at the compound. The last few days they've been coming in, all huddling around one of the tables, whispering to each other. It got so weird that the other night I tried to listen in on what they were talking about, but it didn't do me any good.

As soon as they noticed me hanging around they all shut their mouths tighter than a kid being force fed a forkful of liver."

"Capricorn, have any of your customers mentioned anything interesting?" Aries asked. "You know what they say, 'Pillows hold no secrets'."

Capricorn sat at the table, a cup of coffee in one hand, the other hand shielding her eyes from the light. Her last customer had not left the cabin until nearly six o'clock that morning and she had not yet gone to bed.

"Nothing worth mentioning," she replied in a voice made thick from lack of sleep. "But, if you want, I'll see what I can find out for you, Boss Lady."

Although she would not have been pleased at being called that term by any of the other girls, hearing the words coming from Capricorn helped to heal her lost sense of control. Aries both despised and envied Capricorn. The beautiful woman was only a prostitute, but everything about her was always perfect. If she'd had the woman's looks and her own brains she was certain she could have ruled the world.

"Thank you, Capricorn. Yes, I'd like that. But be careful how you do it. We don't want to raise any red flags. So far we've been able to keep under the town's gossip radar and we need to keep it that way."

* * *

When Aries returned to her room that morning she immediately knew something had changed.

During the last several days every time she stepped through the door a horrible sense of rejection swept over her. If she hadn't been afraid of angering Horace even more than she already had, she would have found somewhere else to sleep.

It had been like this ever since the debacle at Wyntoon. Horace's anger had hit her with such intensity the moment she stepped through the door she was thrown from her feet and left her sprawling.

"Get up!" His rage was so potent she not only heard it, she felt it in her bones.

She rose to her feet, only to feel the pain of his fist slamming into her face, sending her flying backward into the closed door.

"Let me explain!" she gasped.

He responded by grabbing her by the throat and squeezing.

She knew better than to fight him. Her own strength was only human. Her only defense was to let him do as he wished and hope he would let her go before it was too late.

Just as she was slipping into unconsciousness he released her.

Too terrified to rise, she cowered on the floor, waiting for his next attack. She had never known Horace's full wrath before - had not known his anger could be as deadly as his loving was thrilling. Instead of frightening her away, the power she felt in his attack entrapped her even further. She was his willing slave. Her mind mixed the emotions of fear and pleasure to the point she felt she would surely die if he ever left her.

It was that paradox that Horace used to torture her - by withdrawing his presence from her room, by abandoning her soul. Without his essence Aries was left in a cold, airless room. No matter what time of day or night she returned to it, he was not there. She felt powerless to resist the pull of the room, yet while she was in it she could do nothing but sit in the center of the circle and wait. Night after night she prayed to him, begging him to return to her

Sleep was out of the question. He would come back to her. He must! And when he did, he must find her waiting, his adoring slave. She was his vessel. She must wait for him to fill her with his spirit.

As she stepped through the door this time, instead of feeling the dull ache of unrequited passion, she felt Horace's welcoming essence. He enveloped her with his essence. Obeying his wordless command she removed all of her clothes.

Stepping into the center of the Zodiac circle, she tipped her head back and closed her eyes. With outstretched arms she turned her palms upward in a gesture of acceptance.

"I am here, my husband of evil. I am yours and only yours. If it be thy will, I ask you to come to me, to use me, to make me part of you."

She felt her soul slip out of her body, leaving room for him to take possession of her every cell. She gasped aloud as she felt him enter her, filling her body with his essence. In that instant Aries ceased to exist. Only Horace Carpenter remained.

Her mind was his mind now. She no longer had to ask for his direction or permission. Her body, her soul - her everything - were his.

Chapter 37

Horace

Each member of the Sisterhood noted the change in their leader, but no one dared to speak of it. Aries had always been a forceful, strong-minded woman, and she still was. But there was a difference to her force now, something with menacing edge. What they couldn't know, of course, was the Aries they knew was no more. The person who was looking out of her eyes and speaking in her voice was their new leader, Horace Carpenter.

The most noticeable change in her behavior was that she no longer allowed Scorpio to avoid the evening gatherings. "You will join us this evening," she said to Scorpio after the evening meal ended and the other Sisters began to gather in the main living area.

"But I …"

"You will join us … tonight and every night. When you joined this Sisterhood you gave up your past life. You are ours, and we are yours. We are one, now and forever. Now, come!"

More afraid than angry, Scorpio followed Aries into the living room and sank down onto one of the huge pillows that had been placed all around the room. Soothing harp music and musty scented incense filled the room.

She glanced around, checking to see what the other girls were doing so she might copy them. Something told her that if she was smart she would do everything she could to appear to be like them - everything, that is, except she was determined not to ingest the drug Aries was in the process of handing out.

She remembered what it had been like before she'd stopped participating in the evening ritual. Everything seemed so nice then, actually quite lovely - the music, the drugs, the sound of Aries' gentle voice. She participated quite willingly, happy to be a member of the Sisterhood. But after several sessions she begun to question what was happening to her. She could never quite put her finger on what bothered her, but somewhere in the deepest part of her subconscious she knew what Aries was doing was wrong. Now, sitting once again amongst her friends and Sisters, she felt that same emotion.

Following the others, she let herself sink down into the softness of the pillow. Closing her eyes, she followed Aries' directions to take deep breaths and allow herself to find total relaxation. She could hear Aries walking from one woman to another but did not know what she was doing until she felt Aries' hand at her mouth, slipping a tiny pill between her lips. As she listened to Aries step away, she opened one eye just enough to see that Aries was not looking at her. She quickly spit the pill into her hand, then dropped it down the wide neck of her blouse.

When Aries had completed distributing the pills she returned to her seat. The music was quieter now, making it easier for all of the Sisters to hear their leader's soft, monotone voice. Just as Scorpio felt herself slipping under the spell of Aries words she managed to pull her mind back, willing herself to ignore the hypnotic sound.

Aries was wrong. No one owned her, Scorpio thought. Let the others give themselves to Aries and her crazy ideas if they wanted to, but not her!

Scorpio continued to attend the drug-induced hypnotic sessions after that, but always fought silently to resist. Even when she was forced to accept the pill she fought with all her strength to keep Aries out of her head.

* * *

Maybe everything actually did happen for the best, Scorpio thought a few days after Aries had made her rejoin the Sisterhood's regular schedule. If she hadn't, Scorpio would not have been at the breakfast table the morning Leo mentioned something that would eventually turn out to be the most important gossip she had ever gleaned.

"I heard the strangest thing last night," Leo said. "Business was a little slow, so I had time to sit with one of our regulars who lives down by Mott Airport. You know where it is, right? It's that little airport just north of Dunsmuir. Anyway, he said he was up taking a pee in the middle of the night when he heard a bunch of cars driving by his house, going to the runway.

"That little airport is way too small for lights and stuff pilots need to land there at night, so it was real odd for anyone to be driving by that late. Anyway, this guy, Harry, he said he went upstairs where he could get a look at the runway and saw five big black limos at the airport gate. One of the limo drivers got out, unlocked the gate and drove to the end of the field. Right about then a black helicopter, looked like it might be military - he couldn't see markings, but he knows about stuff like that - anyway, it settled down just a little way from the cars. A guy climbs out of it and gets into one of the limos. The 'copter lifted off and two of the cars left, followed by the one the guy from the chopper got into, then the last two left. They were practically bumper-to-bumper when they drove past Harry's house.

"What do you suppose that means? I mean, it must'a been someone real important, don't 'cha think?"

"Did Harry see which way they went?" Aries asked, her full attention directed at Leo.

"Well, he knows they went up on the I-5, but 'cuz of all the trees back of his house, he couldn't actually see which direction they went after that. But he's pretty sure he could hear them driving north."

North, Aries thought, *north as in on the way to Wyntoon?*

Aries rose from the table. "Those limos ... might they be secret service"? Horace couldn't think who else they might be. "And if they are Secret Service, who might they be protecting in the middle of the night up here in Siskiyou County? Who would generate that kind of service besides the President?"

It was at that very instant that his plan came to him full scale. No matter who the guy from the helicopter was, he must be very important to deserve a whole squadron of Secret Service operatives. And there was nowhere anywhere near Dunsmuir other than the Hearst place where a guy that important would be staying at. It all added up to one thing: This was the night the Sisterhood of the Zodiac would stake out their claim in history.

At least that was what he thought after breakfast that day. His plans would change drastically after what he learned from Capricorn when she belatedly got out of bed.

* * *

"You look like shit," Aries said to Capricorn when the beautiful prostitute came stumbling into the kitchen around two o'clock that afternoon. "What did you have, an all-nighter?"

"Something like that," Capricorn said as she poured herself a cup of coffee. "You aren't going to believe who came into Buck's after Leo left last night."

"Let me try," Areas said. "Was it the President?"

"Hey, you're good. But it wasn't him. But you were closer than you might have guessed. "It was his secret lover, that's who."

"Come on, you're kidding us," Libra laughed as she washed out the coffee pot and began putting in fresh grounds.

"I swear to God, it was. And it's a man! I mean, who would have ever imagined?"

Aries was standing perfectly still, taking it all in.

"Turns out, the President is actually having an affair with another man, and he's going to be staying with him tonight right next door to me. I only hope I get to see him!"

A slow smile spread across Aries' face as she said, "Oh, I think we can manage that."

* * *

That evening's hypnosis session was the most intense it had ever been. Scorpio could feel the energy pulsating throughout the room as Aries instructed the Sisters on the coming night's events. She described over and over in explicit detail each member's duty.

"This is what we've all been waiting for," Horace said in Aries' voice, "the time for us to show the world there has never been, nor will there ever be, a force greater than the Sisterhood of the Zodiac. Our names, each and every one of us, will be famous all over the world. And not just for a day, or a month, or even a year. We will be known for all time throughout the entire world as the women who killed the President of the United States and his male lover."

The women all broke out in one loud cheer. All, that is, except for Scorpio, who was so shocked she forgot to imitate the others for a second too long, long enough for her inaction to be noticed by Aries.

* * *

Horace could not believe his good fortune. He had suspected who the night's victim would be, but now he *knew* who it was. No, who they both were!

He could see the next day's headlines now, not just that the President was dead, but that he was killed in the arms of his male lover!

He realized there was more than a good chance that none of them would survive the night's events, but so what? It wasn't exactly as if he was going to die - he'd died decades ago. He would continue on just as he had since the day his 'loving' wife murdered him by sticking a whole swarm of black widow spiders on him. He learned that day that if a person hated strong enough he could hang around planet earth as long as he wanted to. No, he wasn't going anywhere. But a whole lot of others weren't as clever as he was.

Chapter 38

"Good lord, do you think I'd make a joke about something like this? I'm telling you, Aries just told the Sisterhood that we're going to kill the President tonight. I was there! Eddy, what am I going to do?"

"The first thing you're going to do is get in here and close the door. If what you're saying is true we sure as hell don't want anyone to hear us discussing it out here on the stairs. Sound carries a long way in this old building."

What Eddy said was all too true, Aquarius thought as she slipped as quietly as possible back down the stairs. She had been on her way to see if Eddy needed anything else before she went to bed when she heard every word the two had spoken to each other. She'd been feeling sorry for Eddy before she overheard his and Scorpio's conversation. Even though he was not an official member of the Sisterhood, when it was learned what they had done, the simple fact that he lived with them was sure to make him as suspect as the rest of them.

Well, she didn't feel sorry for him now. And she sure as hell didn't feel sorry for that little traitor, Scorpio. When she'd finished telling Aries what she'd just heard Scorpio would be lucky if she lived long enough to see the night's business done.

After listening to Aquarius, Horace did not hesitate an instant. He knew what had to be done and he knew it had to be done immediately.

Making a quick stop at Aries' room to pick up the key to Eddy's apartment, he returned to the living room where he once again spoke to the Sisters in the monotonous tone Aries used during the hypnosis sessions. Although Aries' voice was calm, he wanted to bellow out with rage. He would kill them both before he'd let them ruin everything he'd worked so hard for.

If he didn't do something quickly that little bitch and her whoring bastard friend would spoil everything. He'd be damned to hell if he'd give them the chance.

"Listen to my voice, my Sisters. Listen closely. People who we thought were our friends are plotting at this very moment to keep us from accomplishing our sacred mission. We must stop them. Rise now and come with me. You must make no sound as we go to Eddy's apartment, where I will unlock the door. As soon as the door is unlocked, I will dash in and you must follow me. The first three of us to enter will grab Eddy and hold him down. The next three will hit him on the head with the large iron skillet from our kitchen. The rest of us will do the same with Scorpio."

As he thought about it, he realized this thing with Scorpio and Eddy could work to his benefit. It would give him a chance to see how the girls would respond to his orders. Yes, it was a good thing. In fact, he couldn't think of a better training tool.

Eddy and Nancy were standing in his kitchen, just a step or two away from the doorway when Aries and the others burst into the room. They both turned in shock as what seemed like an army of women stormed into the apartment and swarmed over them. Like a well-oiled machine, each Sister did as she had been instructed. Before either of their victims was able to cry out, they had been pinned to the floor. Though they struggled fiercely each was knocked unconscious in mere moments.

* * *

Eddy was the first to come awake. His head throbbed with pain. The space around him was totally black. Confused and nauseous, he couldn't figure out what the hell had happened.

"Eddy?" Nancy's voice was little more than a whisper.

"Where are you, baby?" he asked.

"I don't know. All I know is, it's dark and cold. I think I'm lying on cement."

"Are you okay?"

"Well, I'm alive, if that's what you mean. But, my head hurts so bad!"

255

By forcing his mind to ignore his own pain, he managed to figure out the direction her voice was coming from. "Stay where you are, sweetheart. I'm coming to get you."

They were only a few feet apart but the journey from where he had been dumped to where she lay seemed to take him forever. When he finally found her, he pulled her into his arms. Holding her close, he patted her back as if she were a small child who needed comforting.

"What happened, Eddy?"

"I don't know. I ... Oh, my God, it was Aries, she and those damned puppets of hers. They attacked us."

"Eddy, they're going to kill those people. She must know I told you and they're going to kill us, too!"

There was nothing he could say to comfort her or assuage her fears. He had no doubt that what she said was true. It wasn't a question of if they would be killed, only of when.

Chapter 39

EMILY

"Emily, wake up!"

She tried to ignore Ada's voice. Would she never let her alone?

"Go away," she groaned as she turned over in bed in a vain effort to ignore the woman who had been coming to her in her dreams every night for the past week. "Let me sleep!"

Suddenly she felt hands on her shoulders, shaking her so hard she nearly fell out of bed. "What the …?" She was awake then, sitting up in bed, her heart pounding so hard she thought it would burst out of her chest.

"You've got to go the mortuary," Ada's voice rang in her ears.

If Emily'd had even a chance of falling back to sleep it was gone now. It was one thing to hear Ada in her dreams, another thing altogether to hear her when she was awake *and* to feel her ghostly hands on her body. Was she losing her mind?

She wished with all her heart that Jim had not taken this week to go off hunting with his friends. When he was with her she rarely if ever had such vivid dreams.

"Ada, what do you want from me?" She felt guilty and fearful at the same time. Ada had been such a wonderful friend. How could she turn her back on her now?

"They're going to kill them, Emily. Get dressed and go … now!"

"Ada, please stop! Go away!"

"Emily, I'm sorry, but there's no one else who can save those two young people. Please, *please* do this for me."

Ada reached out for Emily's hand, holding it gently.

"Have I gone insane, Ada?"

"No, my dear. You're the sanest person I've ever known."

"Then why is this happening to me?"

"Because only you can save those people. If you don't go right now, he's going to kill them all."

Emily turned on the lamp beside her bed. Glancing all around the room, she saw she was alone in the room.

"You're not here, Ada. If you were, I'd see you."

"But I am. And I will continue to be until you do as I ask."

Emily rose from her bed and began to dress. It was insane but she knew in her heart she could not ignore Ada's pleas any longer. If it took going to the mortuary for her to get a good night's sleep, then she might as well get it over with.

Chapter 40

Horace

Horace couldn't decide if it would be better to go ahead and kill Scorpio and Eddy, or if he should wait until after his own Helter Skelter. His first instinct was to just go ahead and get them permanently out of the way. Not only were they no longer of any use to him, they had become liabilities. He really ought to go down to the basement and get it over with.

The only thing that kept him from doing it was the fact that he was basically a very methodical person. He liked doing things in order. Aries' main goal had always been to make a name for herself as being the woman who topped Charlie Manson and he saw no reason not to follow through with her plan. The only way for that to happen would be if the Sisterhood of the Zodiac killed someone who was more famous than Charlie's victims. For some reason it felt like, if he killed Scorpio and Eddy before achieving that objective, it would drain energy away from the ultimate challenge. There were so few hours before the Sisterhood were to fulfill that dream, did he dare risk taking the chance?

Then he realized that if he left them where they were, they would die. In fact, he was killing them this very moment! The room he'd left them in, the embalming room, was hermetically sealed and they would soon suffocate to death for lack of oxygen, and no one would be able to hear their calls for help, either.

The thought of them down there, breathing in their last breaths of air, pleased him. What better way for them to serve his needs? Just knowing they were already suffering gave him a new surge of energy.

Chapter 41

EMILY

It was late when she got there - nearly three o'clock. Grabbing her handbag, she ran up the stairs as quickly as her pregnant body allowed her. Less than two months from her due date, the pounds she had gained were a definite handicap. Fumbling for the keys that had found their way to the bottom of her purse, she cursed the darkness. It took her several tries before she finally found the right key and entered the old building.

Not worrying about whom she might disturb, she ran from one light switch to another until every light on the first floor was glowing. She was shocked at the changes she saw in each room she passed through, but did not worry about any of it. Frankly, she did not care that much what happened to the place. The only thing she cared about now was trying to figure out why Ada had brought her here.

She went from one room to another, from living room to kitchen, from kitchen to dining room, but nothing stood out at her as being particularly sinister.

Finishing with the first floor, she climbed the steps to the second. Once again, she went from room to room, turning on every light, checking out every corner of ever room. These rooms had not been changed as much as those on the first floor, other than the fact they were obviously being inhabited.

But then she came to what she had always thought of as Horace's room, the room Jim had wanted to turn into his office. For her it was the most hated room in the entire building. When she opened the door to that room and turned on the overhead light she knew she had finally found the key to the mystery of why Ada had made her return. The room had been changed, but not like any of the others.

Her eyes were drawn immediately to the center of the floor. A cold chill swept through her as she gazed at the circle that had been painted there. She noted the signs and names of the Zodiac, the unlit candles on the altar, the heavy atmosphere that permeated every square inch of space. She knew without being told that Horace was still part of the room, that his energy had never left it.

"Yes, it is Horace," Ada's voice whispered desperately in her ear. "We must stop him!"

Emily turned from the room, panic etched on her face. "What can we do? What can I do?"

"Hurry! Go to the embalming room. *Now!*"

Emily did not hesitate for a moment. She dashed to the hallway and down the stairs, through the front door and down the outside steps to the entry to the basement.

She yanked desperately at the door, only to discover it was locked. In her haste to unlock it, she managed to drop the keys three times before she was finally able to throw the door open.

Flipping on the overhead light she tried the door of the embalming room, only to find it locked, too.

"Damn, damn, damn," she mumbled.

"The key! Get the key!"

"Ada, damn it! I know you think you're helping, but you've got to stop yelling at me! I'm just about there!"

This time she only dropped the keys twice before she finally had the door open.

Considering all the craziness of the past moments, Emily figured she was beyond being shocked, but she soon discovered this was not true. Nothing in her wildest dreams could have prepared her for what she saw in the small room. There, against the farthest wall was a young man cradling what appeared to be an unconscious teenaged girl. Both of them must have been hit on the head, as the hair on both of their heads was matted with coagulated blood.

"Oh, you poor things!" she moaned as she raced to their side. "Whatever happened?"

"Nancy needs help," the young man whispered. "We need…"

He slumped to his side, his arms still holding onto the girl.

She hated to leave the two victims alone even for a moment but she had no choice. Her best chance of helping them was to run up to Dunsmuir Street to the Sheriff's office. She was there in less than five minutes. In ten minutes more, Eddy and Nancy were being loaded into ambulances and being driven to the hospital.

Emily knew she would have to give the authorities a statement about what she had found but thank God she could wait to get home and have a cup - no, make that a potful - of coffee.

"Go with them … you've got to go with them!"

Emily sat behind the steering wheel and closed her eyes. She didn't know which emotion was stronger, anger or frustration.

"Damn it, Ada, what the hell do you want from me?"

"You've got to save them. You can't stop now!"

"But I have! I've done all I could. It's up to the doctors now."

"You don't understand. It's not just those two young people. Those two are the key to saving the others, don't you see?"

Emily did not see and she didn't think she wanted to.

"Go to the hospital, Emily. That's where you have to be so they can tell you."

"I'm not leaving home until I 've had some coffee and rested for at least an hour. Now, please, Ada, leave me alone!"

"They'll all die! You can't let them die!"

"Oh, for God's sake," Emily groaned, "I'll go, but there's no way anyone's going to let me get near those two kids."

She was wrong, of course. Emily learned later that from the moment Eddy awoke in the emergency room he had insisted on talking to her. He didn't know her name, or even who she was. All he knew was he had to speak to her as quickly as possible. For some reason his gut feeling was that she would understand his crazy story even though everyone else would think he was a raving lunatic.

"Are you the lady who found those kids?" the woman at the reception desk asked Emily as soon as she stepped through the hospital's main door.

Before Emily could even say that, yes, she was, the woman said, "Come with me," and led her down the hall to the doors leading to emergency.

A women dressed in scrubs appeared beside Emily and ushered her to one of the curtained-off beds. She was just lowering herself onto a chair that had been placed beside the bed when the young man she had found in the mortuary began talking.

"You've got to tell them I'm not crazy," he said to her. "The cops, they won't listen to me. They think my head's messed up. But it's not! I know what I'm talking about!"

"Listen to him, Emily. He knows what he's saying." Ada's voice urged.

"Okay, I'm listening."

"There's a gang of crazy women down in Castella. They're going to kill the President." He must have seen doubt in Emily's eyes, because he suddenly became quite agitated. "It's happening now! Oh, my God, don't you understand? It's happening now!"

Reaching out to comfort him she said, "I believe you. If you'll lie back down, I'll go talk to the Sheriff's deputy."

"But ..."

"I know you think they won't listen to me, but I promise I won't let them alone until they do. Now, lay back. I'll be back, but not until I'm sure the Sheriff believes me and sends out a team of deputies, okay?"

Chapter 42

ARIES/HORACE

He watched the Sisters scatter into the darkness. It felt as if each cell in Aries' body had gone into high gear the moment he and the Sisters left the VW bus hidden in the trees and began their silent search. This was what he was made for! Holding the machete ready, he crept toward the small stone cottage where the President of the United States and his lover slept.

Suddenly the entire area was flooded with the light of what appeared to be hundreds of flashlights. Men were yelling, women screamed, and the sound of rapidly firing guns exploded all around him.

With no more use for her body, Horace slipped out of it. It was Aries' party from here on out.

Noooo! Not now!

She would have said the words aloud but they were still in her brain when she was cut down by a volley of bullets. As she sank to the ground, the very last thought that went through her mind was, *I may not have finished the job, but the world will know I had more guts than Charlie Manson. I was going to be the one who killed …*

* * *

The world never learned of the Sisterhood of the Zodiac. Not one word was ever mentioned in any newspaper or television report that there had been an attempt on the President's life, nor were any bodies found in Castella. As far as the rest of the world knew the entire event simply did not happen.

What Aries would never know, in turn, was that she and her followers were thwarted by something as simple as a telephone call. Emily was as good as her word; she did speak to the Sheriff's deputy. And the deputy, not believing for an instant the beat-up guy in the hospital bed knew what he was talking about, decided to cover his ass by calling the number he had for the Secret Service whom he had been informed were currently over at the Hearst compound. He figured, although it didn't seem likely, if the Secret Service *was* there, it was possible the President might actually be there, too.

As far as the President being down at Castella? Well, he'd believe that when he saw it.

The security team did what it was trained to do: Not only was the attack at Castella thwarted, but the attackers and the attack itself simply disappeared. The President and his 'friend' were never in any danger of being either killed or exposed. And the attackers, since they never existed, were never heard of again.

Charlie Manson retained his preeminence as the most hated man in the United States.

Chapter 43

Epilogue

Emily was right back to where she started - trying to figure out what the heck she was going to do with that damned haunted mortuary. Only, now she had the help of her two new friends.

"More coffee, Nancy?" she asked one of her houseguests.

"Please," Nancy replied with the sweetest smile Emily had ever seen.

"And you, Eddy?"

"No, I've had enough." He started to rise from the table but Emily held him back with a touch of her hand.

"If neither of you mind, I'd like sit here for a while and discuss what the future might hold for all of us, before the baby wakes up."

The two young people glanced at one another, then back at their hostess.

"I guess you're wondering when you can get rid of us," Eddy finally said. "You and Dr. Jim have taken care of us a lot longer than either one of us thought you ought to."

"Ought to, as in we didn't have a choice in the matter? Because if that's what you thought, you're dead wrong. No, we brought you here to stay at our house because I need you guys every bit as much as you may of needed me. All three of us needed some healing time and I suspect we all need healing for the same reason."

Seeing the confused expressions on both of their faces, Emily realized it was time for her to tell them the sordid history of Dunsmuir's old mortuary.

"You two were not the first to suffer from living in that house. That building is haunted by one of the most vicious entities who has ever existed. And now I think it's time for you to learn the truth about the spirit of Horace Carpenter."

Emily was interrupted several times while she took care of her brand new daughter. She didn't want to leave any of it out: How Horace married an innocent young girl; how he betrayed her over and over again; and how he eventually murdered their child whom he had refused to call his own. She told them how his wife, when she discovered he'd killed their son, decided she had no choice but to murder him.

"His tormented, twisted spirit never left that building. Ada spent the rest of her life protecting others from his viciousness by staying in the building. It was the only way she knew to keep him under control. When she died, she left the building, and the responsibility of protecting others from Horace, to me.

"Unfortunately, I was not strong enough for the task. I'm as certain as I am alive that everything that happened to those who crossed Horace Carpenter's path since Ada died is my fault. I failed you all."

"But what could you have done?" Nancy cried.

"That's just it - I didn't know what to do. I still don't. That's a burden and a responsibility I will carry with me for the rest of my life."

"You're not carrying it alone, Miss Emily," Eddy said. Leaning across the table, he took both of her hands in his. "If you hadn't come to our rescue Nancy and I would have died in that room. It would have been a horrible, horrible way to die. But you did come. As far as I'm concerned, I'll be right here at your side, helping you in any way I can to get rid of that guy!"

"Me, too, Miss Emily. I don't have anywhere else to call home. I'm staying right here in Dunsmuir. Heck, I've got a good job with people who have offered to let me stay with them for as long as I want. And now I've got you and Dr. Jim and baby Stacy. I'm not going to let any creepy old ghost make me leave the best home I've ever known."

And so it was that people who couldn't have been more different from one another somehow managed to become a family - a family bent on protecting not only each other but every other citizen of their chosen 'home town.'

End Note

In 2012, in a book entitled 'Nixon's Darkest Secrets, Don Fulsom, a former United Press International Washington bureau chief, claimed that President Richard Nixon had conducted a gay affair with a gangster-connected financier called Charles 'Bebe' Rebozo.

The evidence for the affair was about as shady as Mr. Rebozo himself, and there is no indication that either of them visited Castella at any time, but this part of the story was inspired by a persistent rumor that President John F. Kennedy and Marilyn Monroe did indeed have a secret assignation, for three days in 1962, in Castle Stone Cottage #3 in Castella.

Locals reported chatting with Ms. Monroe for over an hour in the now-defunct Mike's Bar in Castella, where she signed a mirror before being picked up by a large limousine in the back of which the distinctive outline of President Kennedy was clearly visible.

Today, all of the five Castle Stone Cottages in Castella are available for holiday rental by contacting Cave Springs Motel and Cabins, Dunsmuir:

4727 Dunsmuir Avenue

Dunsmuir, CA 96025

(888) 235-2721 | (530) 235-2721

Made in the USA
San Bernardino, CA
25 October 2013